MAN ALONE

His name was Regan. They called him the killer cop. He was accused of taking a bribe, and then murdering the man who gave it to him. The jury said he wasn't guilty—but his friends and his colleagues weren't convinced.

So Regan had to prove it all over again— starting with the broad who poured him into a cab that fateful night. She was a big, beautiful redhead from a high class bordello, and when he found her, she was dead as doornails.

TWO TOP

SPILLANE THRILLERS . . .

<u>Killer Mine, Man Alone</u> . . .

published for the first time in the U. S., with that specialty that only Mickey can deliver— the slam-in-the-gut surprise at the finishing kill!

mickey spillane

KILLER MINE

A SIGNET BOOK

Published by The New American Library

SIGNET TRADEMARK REG. U.S. PAT. OFF. AND FOREIGN COUNTRIES
REGISTERED TRADEMARK—MARCA REGISTRADA
HECHO EN CHICAGO, U.S.A.

SIGNET BOOKS are published by
The New American Library, Inc.,
1301 Avenue of the Americas, New York, New York 10019

FIRST PRINTING, JUNE, 1968

PRINTED IN THE UNITED STATES OF AMERICA

CONTENTS

There are times when stories
should be told—even if
some incidents must be
magnified—and some deleted.
To those
I worked with—it was
quite an experience. Thanks.

M. S.

KILLER MINE

KILLER MINE

CHAPTER ONE

I GOT out of the car slowly and stood looking up at the darkened window of the apartment. The cold rain pelted the glass, making it look like a black mirror, an evil, nasty eye in the face of an evil, nasty building. There was something disgusting about it all, something foul and dirty, even unthinkable.

Up there, behind that darkened window, I had to kill myself. Up there I'd know what it would be like to lie dead, know the feeling and sight of featureless expression, the laxity of death.

The gun in my pocket seemed to be too heavy, so I just took it out and crossed the street with it in my hand. The front door was open. So was the inside one. Behind it was the yawning, cavernous mouth of the pitch-black stairway and corridor.

One flight up and to the front.

In my mind I was picturing my face on the floor, half turned into the light, eyes partially opened and jaw slack. All consciousness gone. All conscience gone too. Nothing left. Just dead.

Under my feet the carpet was worn, and each step up brought a musty, aged smell closer. From habit born long ago I stepped over the step that had pulled away from the wall, and as a kid would, counted my way toward the landing.

Four more to go. Then three, two, one and I was there. The door was ten feet away. I didn't hurry. I wasn't in a hurry to see what I looked like dead.

So I went slowly and when I had the knob under my hand I cocked the .38 and thought how stupid it all was. And how it started. In a way it had two starting points, but the first was last and the last first. At the last second I was thinking back over the simplicity and stupidity of the whole thing.

* * *

It was ten minutes after the kill when I got there. The

squad car men were taking statements from the handful who had heard the shots and were trying to make sense from the henna head nighthawk who had seen the car.

The captain was there, an uptown inspector and one of the lab specialists I had seen around a few times. As I got out of the car the photogs were taking their last pics and scrounging for an identification of the dead man.

When I reached the doctor he was just getting up, stuffing the last of his instruments back in his bag. I said, "How'd he get it?"

"Two in the chest and one in the neck, any one fatal."

"He say anything before he died?"

He shook his head. "Not a thing. I knew he was dying and I tried to bring him around long enough to say something. Couldn't do it."

"Tough."

The doctor drew in his breath and made a wry face. "It was bound to happen." He scanned the block, taking in the stone faces of the tenements. "Anything can happen here. This is typical."

I watched him without saying anything, then glanced down at the dead man. There wasn't much to see. Blood obscured his face, and on the sidewalk like that he looked small and pitiful, not at all important enough to be knocked off in such spectacular fashion. I looked again, frowned, shook my head at what I thought.

Before I could think on it any longer I heard, "Joe . . . Hey Joe." Captain Oliver was waving at me, his cigar making a red arc in the night. I walked over and nodded. "This is Inspector Bryan, Joe. . . . Lieutenant Joe Scanlon, sir."

Bryan stuck out his hand and grabbed mine. He was a big, beefy cop who had come up the hard way and knew all the ropes that went with the job. "Ollie told me about you, Joe. I asked to have you up here."

"I wondered why the call."

"You know this area?"

"I was born a couple blocks away. It stinks, but I know it."

The inspector pulled on his cigarette. "You up on current events around here?"

Before I answered I tried to see what he was getting to but couldn't make it. I said, "Partly. No details."

"You know the dead man?"

I squinted at him, then: "You make him?"

"Not yet. We're waiting on prints."

The funny feeling came back and I couldn't shake it off. I turned, went back to the corpse, took a good, close look and stood up. "Forget prints. I can make him."

"Who is he, Joe?" Oliver asked.

"Doug Kitchen. We grew up together."

"Positive make?"

I nodded. "Positive. He used to run with my sister. A nice guy. No punk."

The inspector flipped the butt and said, "Nice guys don't get shot like that."

"This one did."

"Nuts." His eyes got too cold and knowing.

I said, "My old man got gut shot by a cop on the next corner. He was mistaken for somebody else. The cop thought he had a gun. He was carrying his thermos bottle."

"So?"

"So Doug was no punk. I knew him. That's enough."

"What's he doing out at four-thirty in the morning?"

"You check the corpse, Inspector?" I didn't say it nice.

"Briefly."

"Then maybe you noticed his shipyard badge. He was on the eight to four and coming home."

"My slip," Bryan said. He grinned at me then. "Something's happening around here, Joe. Four crazy, yet well-planned kills in one month. None of them tie in except that they're all executed in the same area. It doesn't set right. I think we need a local man to take it on."

"Me?"

"You lived here. You know the people."

"Only the old ones. Things change."

"I know. We want to keep them from changing."

"It can't be that big."

"Four murders, with three from the same gun, can be big," he said. "It can go to more." He reached in his pocket and pulled out a lined index card. He handed it to me and held a light on it. "Know the names?"

After I looked at them I said, "I know them."

"Well?"

"We were kids then. We went to the same school together. I was a hell of a lot older than most of them."

"But it's a pattern."

"Of a sort maybe. The dead men lived within ten blocks of each other."

"And all killed pretty quick, one after the other."

I handed the card back. "What do I do?"

Bryan grinned that old cop grin of his. "You take it on."

"Get off it, friend."

He gave me that grin again. "You won't be creamed. You got a girl down the block. It'll all look pretty natural."

"I don't have any girl."

13

"You will have before long, mister. She's a dame you knew as a kid and as far as anybody is concerned around here you've met accidentally again and are just picking up all the old pieces."

"Listen, Inspector, I don't want any dame messing around."

"Maybe you will after you've seen this one."

"Oh, for . . ."

"Her name's Marta Borlig. Remember her?"

I couldn't help the face I made. "Sure," I said disgustedly.

"She's a policewoman now, but nobody around here knows it. It's all in the department and you can keep it that way. That's how you like it anyway."

"You know a lot about me."

"We looked long and carefully into this thing, Joe. Now listen. It's small and slummy but it's got some nasty overtones. If it happened to all punks or known criminals we could do it routine, but now we got citizens involved who don't like murder in their back yards. They own stores and work hard. They have the right of complaint. Soon the papers catch on and we're targets."

I nodded. "And if I don't produce, I'm the target."

"That's the general idea, Joe."

"Then go blow it. I won't play. I don't feel like being a target. It happened too many times for me to ask for it."

"You're being told, Joe."

"Swell, so I'm told. You want me to pull strings? I've been around a long time too."

"Okay, boy. You call it."

"Not me, Inspector. Not me. I don't work into real upper echelons. I'm a cop, plain and simple. But I'm just cop enough to blow off a job I don't want to get fixed into."

Captain Oliver said, "Joe . . ."

It was a long time before I tied myself together, then I grinned and said, "Okay, okay. I'll sucker myself. I'll be a real slob." My grin got bigger then. "But the first boy that doesn't back me up gets chopped. Quick and hard. Understood?"

"Sure," Bryan said. "Now stick around. We want that killer."

"Suppose we hit politics?"

Bryan's grin was an even bigger one. "No matter who or how," he said.

Then he walked off and I was standing there by myself.

Downtown was ready for me. The desk sergeant spotted me coming in, got up and introduced himself as Nick Rossi, then had me meet the rest of the shift that was still there.

From the curiosity in their faces I could see that somebody had given them a build up on the deal.

The sergeant took my arm and pointed to the room behind the desk. "We have the files drawn and sitting on the desk. There's more stuff in those six folders than Hoover had on Capone."

"Six?"

"The Kitchen job was just completed. Bryan said to have it ready by this morning."

"He didn't give you much time."

"Two days, but it was enough. Hell, the guy was clean. Only offense was a drunk charge in '46. You can get through the clean ones easy."

"I hope I can do it just as fast."

"This a big one, Lieutenant?"

"Who knows. You have a look at the reports?"

"Only the index cards when I pulled them. Kitchen's I went over."

"Marty . . ."

"Send Marty in," I said.

When he went out I closed the door, turned on the fan and sat down. The .38 riding my hip in a Weber rig was uncomfortable, so I sprung it out and laid it on the edge of the desk.

Rossi wasn't far off in his description of the dossiers. They were thick with everything that included birth, graduation and death certificates. In each were ballistics and kill photos and what little data there was surrounding the crime. That was as far as the police detail went. The rest was a compilation of every event that transpired in a person's life. A lot of it was familiar to me, and in each one my own name showed up in the pre-report briefs.

Like a cast of characters, I thought. A damn play.

The phone rang and I picked it up and said, "Scanlon, homicide."

The voice on the other end was deep, yet soft. "Commissioner Arbatur speaking, Lieutenant. Is everything satisfactory there?"

I let out a soundless whistle. This was the hurry-hurry boy on the other end. "Fine, Commissioner. We just got rolling. I'm going over the reports now."

"That's good." He sounded too damn paternal.

I said, "How far up does this thing go?"

"Quite far, Lieutenant. I imagine you are getting the picture?"

"Well . . . so far each kill has been an individual item for the sheets. No press boy tied them in."

"Then the gun is our secret."

"And if it slips out?"

"Panic, Lieutenant. You know that. A killer is having a field day in an area where there are twenty thousand strong pro-administration voters."

My voice got real edgy. "Tell you what, Commissioner," I said, "tell the voters to go shove it. You too. I'm after a killer. He's got only certain potential victims. They're the ones I'm concerned about. Not voters. Not even you. Got that?"

"Lieutenant . . ."

"Shove it, Commissioner. Brace me once and I'll bump the sheets. They'll tear you apart and I'll help them. Stay out of my hair."

Before he could answer I hung up. Outside, a few mouths would be open around the switchboard and in the commissioner's office the word would go around fast. But I wasn't kidding. I never did like political appointees who came out of cloak and suit shops.

So now I had a killer and a politician to buck. Great. Just great.

I went back to the reports and started sifting through them. I used the gun as a paperweight to keep the fan from blowing them around and had it in my hand when there was a rap on the door. I yelled, "Come on in."

And a startling voice said, "Going to shoot me with it, Joe?"

She wasn't just tall. She was great big. She was honey blonde with the mark of the Valkyrie and her mouth was curved in a moist, lush grin because my eyes swept over her so fast. Her body seemed to want to explode, and only the tailored suit kept it confined.

My mind kept reaching, but I couldn't quite make her, then she said, "Plainclotheswoman Marta Borlig reporting, Lieutenant," and the grin got even bigger.

"Well, whatta ya know." It was all I could think of to say.

"You might tell me how much I've grown," she smiled, "everybody always does."

"Might say you filled out a little too."

She walked toward me, her hand out, and I stood up and took it. "Nice to see you again, Joe," she said. She only had to look up a little bit to meet my eyes.

"So you're Marty."

"I'm Marty. But we keep it quiet. Joe. Special detail."

"Now how the heck can you be kept quiet? You're bait for anything that's got eyeballs."

16

"I understand you didn't exactly relish me as an assistant," she said impishly.

"My memory was twenty years old." I looked at her again, unable to take my eyes from her. "Little Giggie."

"Don't let's dredge that name up again." She strode to the aged leather chair by the wall and folded up into it. For a girl so big she had the lazy poise of a fat cat. "I often wondered what happened to you, Joe."

"Very little." I dropped into my chair and leaned back. "Two years of college, the force, the war and back on the force again. Study hard, work up the ladder. You know."

She squinted at me, puzzled. "No home life?"

"No wife, if that's what you mean. Never had time, I suppose." I let out a short laugh. "Now, if we're supposed to be playing footsies, what does your old man do to help the act?"

"Old man?"

"Well, I don't feel like being a corespondent in a divorce suit, kiddo. I'd sooner he had a script."

The smile started at the corners of her eyes and reached her mouth a few seconds later. It was a lopsided laugh, full of humor. "I think we can ad lib this one, Joe. You see . . . I'm sort of a spinster lady."

"Oh, no," I said.

"Oh, yes," she laughed. "I seem to overwhelm people. I scare them."

"I'm strangely unafraid," I laughed back.

"That's because you always were a clod. Clods don't think, scare easily or get married. You're a big, ugly clod. How big are you, Joe?"

"Six-two. Weight, two-oh-two, age, up there as you damn well know. How about you?"

"Three inches smaller, four years younger and forty-two pounds lighter."

"At least it'll be a big team. We can tear the top off things."

"Just like the old days," she mused. "What happened to everybody?"

I stared out the window and shrugged. "Gone. If they had any sense they got out. All eleven kids in my family took off. The three youngest can't even be located."

Her eyes had a faraway look in them. "And Larry . . . do you hear from him?"

"Chief Crazy Horse," I said softly. "No, he's gone . . . someplace. We met once during the war. It was by accident and we were both drunk. You can guess how that was."

"You were funny brothers, Joe." She curled her feet farther under her. "Who was the oldest?"

"He was."

"Chief Crazy Horse," she repeated. "Those were the days. It was a fight just to stay alive. I can remember when eating was a luxury, not to be taken too lightly."

"And your family, Marty?"

"The folks died. Young Sed is in college trying hard to be a dentist."

"Still living in the same place?"

Marta nodded. "For some silly reason I forgot to move. The folks owned the building, you know, and it was convenient with Sed needing funds." She gave me that big grin again. "That's our base of operations, I understand."

"That's what I hear."

"I'll buy a couch so we can sit and talk."

"Forget it. Get a bigger icebox instead."

"You sound just like a lousy cop. All stomach and no heart."

"That's me, chicken." I grinned back and said, "Let's get under these reports. I need some filling in."

"Yes, sir. Yes, sir, Lieutenant, sir."

* * *

At six we had sandwiches sent up, and at ten we stacked the folders back in the files. I turned the fan off, stuck the .38 back in the Weber holster and said, "Let's get some coffee. Real china-cup coffee without a cardboard taste."

Marta put her jacket back on, buttoned it and picked up her purse. "Are we off duty, Lieutenant?"

"Off duty."

"Then hello, Joe."

A laugh twisted its way out of me.

"No wonder you went up so fast. You're a symbol of devotion to service and stark purity." Then she reached out and took my hand. "But you're nice, Joe. Where to for coffee?"

"Down the block. It's the closest."

Ray made his money from the oversize urn. It seemed to be all he sold, but at least he was in the right location for it. If he didn't need a table to do his paper work on he wouldn't have had the one in the back. To him the counter was the thing. We picked up our mugs and went back to the corner table and sat down.

I said, "We didn't learn much, did we?"

"Not unless you like biographies." She paused and put her cup down. "Joe . . . do you make anything of it?"

"Something's there," I nodded. "You helped compile those statistics, didn't you?"

"That's right. You saw the woman's touch?"

"It was a little flowery."

"They asked for that. They wanted every detail. They thought there had to be a background tie-in someplace. There certainly wasn't any other connection."

I blew on my coffee slowly, watching her over the rim of it. "Let's boil it down real quick, Marty. Let's get one common denominator first."

She made circles on the table with the wet bottom of the cup. "The gun. The same .38 killed them all."

"What else?" I asked her.

She was real sharp. She picked up one skipped detail right away. "Single shot each. Fatal almost immediately. Indicates professional killer. Doug Kitchen was the exception. He was shot on the run and the third bullet was merely insurance for the first two. Further professionalism."

I nodded. "That's a common detail, but not the denominator. Now involve us too and you'll see what I mean."

Her face was impassive a moment, then she got the point. "You and I knew them all, didn't we." It was a statement rather than a question.

"Curious, isn't it?"

"In a way . . . at least from a coincidental standpoint. It was your neighborhood and still is mine. That's why we're on this one."

"You haven't hit it, kid. You'll never make sergeant this way."

"I don't get it."

"Then I'll wait until you do," I told her.

"Smart guy," she said. "Just because you can pull rank."

I grinned at her. "Now you sound like old Giggie herself."

Her eyes flashed quickly. "Listen. . . ."

I waved a finger at her. "You watch it, kid, or I'll start issuing orders. Then you'll have to do whatever I tell you."

The laughter came back in her face again. "Like what?"

"You'd be surprised at what I might order you to do."

"I wouldn't be surprised at all," she grinned back. "Just don't leave the lights on."

"Damn dames," I grunted. "Even when you're policemen you can't forget you're dames." Then we both laughed and got up and split the check and went back to the office.

CHAPTER TWO

I LOOKED across the desk at Marty, wondering at the size of her and the wild chestnut color of her hair, wondering why such a broad should go cop when she could lay the world at her feet with the *big look*. The resiliency of youth whom so many desired had been replaced by the lushness of maturity, whose desire was superior, and only obtainable by certain few.

I was grinning when she looked up and said, "You're philosophizing. I can tell."

"How?"

"You look smug."

"It doesn't happen often. Let me enjoy the moment."

Her smile started gently, then broadened when some subtle intuition gave her an insight into my thoughts.

"Let me," she said softly. "Please?"

The seconds that passed were years going back and little things coming forth.

"What are you thinking?"

"When you were the *Big Pig* because you wanted to be the cop and Polack Izzie and you got into the fight over me."

"We didn't fight over you."

"You did, friend," she reminded me. "It was night and I was coming home from the library when he jumped me next to the Strauss store."

I laughed because I remembered all too painfully. "He beat the hell out of me, chicken."

"Sure he did," she chuckled, "but I got away. I never did thank you, did I?"

"Never."

"So thanks."

"Don't bother. We didn't fight over you. He ran over my foot with that old Packard 120. You happened along at the right time."

"Don't be modest, Joe. You fought over me."

"Old Giggie?"

"Well . . . maybe you knew how I'd wind up."

Both of us laughed at that one day so long ago. The laugh was real short, then she bent her head down into the reports again and I looked at the wild chestnut hair and felt real funny inside.

Real funny.

Both of us playing guns for public money and winding up on the same deal.

Sergeant Mack Brissom rapped on the door and walked in, grinning at the comfortable little scene. "Kind of late, ain't it?"

I shrugged. "Got to get it done. You have the rest of the stuff?"

He tapped the envelope. "It's all here. A lot of speculation, but it can count. You know how those things are."

"Sure."

"You want me to brief you?"

"Yeah, but *in* brief. You know? Sit down." I leaned back in the chair and folded my hands behind my head. "Let's hear it."

Mack bit the end off a cigar, spit the piece into his palm and lit up. It stunk, but it was part of the mores of the place.

"Well, you know the guys who were knocked off. René Mills, Hymie Shapiro, 'Noisy' Stuccio and Doug Kitchen."

"I knew them when we were kids."

"You see the ballistics report on Kitchen?"

I shook my head no.

"Same gun, so now the heat is really on. Bryan says hurry -hurry. Anyway, they all got rap sheets except this Kitchen guy and on him there's nothing. The rest were backtracked down to when they were still playing hookey, but if you can tie them in to each other you're better'n I am. You went over the earlies, didn't you?"

"In detail."

"Make anything?"

I shook my head again. "Nothing there but a familiarization course. What's the word from outside?"

"Well . . ." He reached forward and picked a sheet from the envelope and scanned it quickly, then flipped it back. "McNeil . . . he's on the beat there . . . he knew them. René Mills and Stuccio had been sharing a pad a month earlier, then René hit a daily double and moved out. McNeil figured Mills was running numbers when he was bumped and he knew damn well Noisy was getting bread by pimping for a couple of tomatoes he had on the top floor over old Papa Jones' store. But lately, nobody could tie them in. Both had been playing it quiet enough to be let alone."

"No talk along the street?" I asked him.

"Hell, who'll talk? The few who would, had nothing to say. But anyway, that's your bit now. You're real home town, huh?"

Marty looked up and grinned. "Both of us."

"Yeah, I heard," he said. Then he looked at me and winked through the haze of smoke. "It pays to be brass. That it does. A chick like this in the department and they yank her all the way across town to be your buddy. Cripes, you shoulda seen the partners they gave me. Old Grootz, fat as a pregnant cow . . . Billy Menter who could say 'yup' and 'nope' and that was all, and one time a matron who looked like my aunt in Linden, but at least that only lasted one day."

"I'm going to stretch this one out," Marty said. I glanced at her and grunted. So did Mack. "Why not?" she said seriously. "Until now it was all juvenile. Wouldn't even put me out in the field where the dips were working."

Mack and I looked at each other and laughed.

"What's so funny about that?" she demanded.

"You," I told her. "I can see you trying like hell to be inconspicuous. Anyway, baby, you were good enough to save for the big one."

Mack laughed again and Marty made a face at me.

I said to Mack, "We're going to play this one on the cool side. They laid out the pattern before they gave it to me, and it might work. I'd sooner go after this chappie through regular channels, but someplace along the line politics got involved and you know district captains can raise a stink, specially when he can pull five thousand votes."

"Well, it happens. What can you do?"

"Marty still lives in the old neighborhood. Nobody knows she's in the department. In that neighborhood it doesn't make for a good rep."

"I know."

"So I court her." I grinned at Marty and she smiled back.

"Things can get mighty interesting in the line of duty," Mack said.

In a stage whisper Marty said, *"I hope!"* and we all laughed.

For some crazy reason all the tension was gone and I had a fat lazy feeling like I used to have back on the beat when it was a hello to everybody and the kids still played stickball and not switchblades and you liked your job, even at the end of the day when your feet hurt but you weren't really tired.

"So what do you think, Mack?"

"It's a toughie. There're nineteen stoolies who put in their two bits out of which we got nothing. The only tie-in is that they were knocked off with the same gun, presumably in the same hand. All neat jobs, no stray shots and strictly big-time pro. The slugs were all .38 specials out of the same box. The lab could check the lube left on each slug."

"That's calling it."

"But that's all they're calling, Joe. You can go through those reports all week and still be out in the bleachers."

"It figures. That's why they're making a damned federal case out of it."

Mack got up and tapped the inch of ash off his cigar into the tray on my desk. "You be careful, Joe. I don't like this one."

"I don't either."

"You know why?"

"No. Clue me."

"Some rumbles been coming out of there lately. That Phil Borley extortion thing. Nobody knew he had left Chi until he muffed this operation here. Then that mob business. Nothing's come of it yet, but the word is that a few of the uptown crowd have been hanging around in strange places. Those lads are working close to the politicos. The campaigning starts early nowadays."

Across from me, Marta frowned in concentration, taking it all in.

"If these kills are inside an organization," Mack said, "you're pushing a big one. If they're outside, the organization won't like their field having a light turned on it and might try to clean up the deal themselves. Either way, you can get caught in a pocket."

I grinned at him. "Don't worry so much. I've been around some."

Mack nodded. "Okay, you know what you can do with that reputation of yours. Always some punk ready to take you on from behind. What I don't like is you going it alone. It just ain't S.O.P."

"Neither is this case."

"You been assigned any help?"

"Just Marty. The rest gets played by ear."

Marta leaned back and crossed her arms. "We can always yell for the beat cop."

"Great," Mack said. "Anyway, if it gets too cozy, a few of us who know that strip can hang around in our spare time."

"Thanks. I might need something like that."

"Sure. You yell. Now, anything you want from our section?"

"I don't think so." I tapped the envelope on the desk. "Thanks for this."

He winked, waved at Marty and sauntered out. On the wall the clock passed the midnight mark and I said, "Enough, kid. Let's shut up shop."

"We're on it, then?" When I nodded she added, "Now what?"

I said, "Now the courtship begins," and leered at her the best way I knew how.

* * *

We waited until Saturday to start the pitch. We let Marta get it going by passing the word to old lady Murphy upstairs and Mr. Clehoe who ran the corner delicatessen that she had met me near where she worked and saw me a couple of times for lunch. It didn't take long for the news to get around that Marta had picked up the pieces with old Pig Scanlon, the cop, and already she was getting dirty looks from anybody at all who had been in the can.

Normally she had Saturdays off, but spent the morning taking a course in Spanish. But as far as the street knew she had a five-and-a-half-day week in an office someplace, so nothing was out of order when we came out of the subway and started toward her place.

At the corner where my old man was shot down I touched her arm and we stopped so I could look around. It had been a long time. Many moons. Many suns. I looked up the street and knew instinctively what lay behind every dirty brownstone front and the way the clothes looked hanging in the alleys behind and could smell the pigeons on the roof.

Resurrecting memories of youth comes easy. You can slip back fast to the old days when life was hot pavement, new sneakers and a nickel in your pocket. The guy who died on the beach at Anzio is a pug-nosed guinea again and he's your best friend. The kid with the lisp next door died up at Ossining two years ago for a gang kill, but for the moment you're ten once more and sharing leads in the class play. The mother of the girl whom you first loved on a sultry rooftop and fought for in the streets below sobs softly at night because the girl is rich and notorious, yet still beautiful despite the channels of whoredom she swam to reach her port of money. But you think of her as lovely, and at fifteen endowed with all those things important to men and boys. You think of Giggie and smile because she was bigger than you were and tougher than most of the kids and sure as hell slated for the school at Hudson if she got caught with you on a stamp into the *Hub's* turf two blocks over. You remember old Larry whom they used to call Chief Crazy Horse and Sam Staples they called Bad Bear when the gang crawled around the eroded rocks playing Indians on the West Side of Central Park.

And I was the Pig. *Big Pig* they called me because I always wanted to play the cop.

24

Mischelle Stegman, the hood from the corner, would laugh when they hosed me about wanting to be in the blue uniform, then one day I saw him mug old Jew Jenkins and take off with his roll and I was the only one who would talk up. Two days after he was subpoenaed, Stegman's buddies took me out of my hallway and went to teach me a lesson. The cop on the beat came along and chewed two of them up and the one who was about to belly-hook him with a switcher suddenly had his back broken by a kid jumping from the stoop railing.

Me.

The slobs shot their mouths off after that, but nobody touched me. They saw to that down at the precinct house.

Then in time it was me on the beat where I had wanted to be for so long. I was off the street and everything looked good. Until the war came. But that passed too, and for a while things were changed. You work, you study, you take tests, a couple of lucky breaks and a couple you sweated for make you a big one on the force with a crazy reputation of hating the politicos and the chiselers and the punks and everybody is scared shitless of you because they can give you nothing and you can slice them every which way. Suddenly the caucus room boys with the thick cigars and thicker bank-rolls come to you simpering and smiling because you're a big one now who doesn't give a yell for the cloak and suiters or the guinea mafia or ignorant spics or the dutchmen or the micks or S.N.C.C. or any of them who play it sidewise because they're strictly all alike in the rule book. Strictly.

Marta said, "Still the same?"

I snapped out of it, realizing that a frown had pulled my eyes into a tight squint. "Essentially."

"You've never been back?"

"I've never wanted to come back." I looked at her and took her arm. "I didn't know about you, Giggie."

"Would it have made a difference?"

I shrugged, but she knew it might have and grinned back. Then we waited for the light to change again and crossed over to the slop chute everybody called Donavan's Dive.

You smelled Donavan's place before you got inside. It had an oldness about it, a hangover from the speakeasy days, an air-conditioned mustiness of stale smoke and staler beer. The side entrance let you into a dining room of sorts, the front one directly to the bar.

There wasn't much room at the bar, just one space about a foot wide where you could sidle in to pick up a drink. The wise guy who saw me steer Marta toward it scrunched around to block it up neatly and the back bar mirror showed a couple of grins.

When the wise guy suddenly and quietly tried to scream from the short hook to the kidney and spilled his drink across the mahogany, the grins stopped. I pulled him away and he staggered to the wall where he tried to catch his breath.

Marta smiled nicely, the guy next to her gave up his stool and we each had a big, cool Pabst in a clear glass mug that made the trip across town worth waiting for.

When the surly faced bartender came back to catch all the details I knew it had come.

It was big and fat with a cigar stuck in the middle of his mouth and his pants carried low under his belly. Somebody had knocked his nose out of line a long time ago, but must have paid for it the hard way. This was the voice of local authority. This was *the man*. With a derby he'd have been the perfect caricature of the old-style ward heeler. Today they call them captains.

He said, "Hey, cop," and when I looked around he shifted the cigar with a tongue roll to the other corner. "You looking to get your badge lifted, you're in the right place. You know that?"

I grinned at him and felt Marta touch my arm lightly. "No, I didn't know that."

One big thick forefinger came up to emphasize the point against my chest. It's one of the things I can't stand at all. It's something a hell of a lot of people learned never to do. The second he touched me I grabbed, twisted and broke it straight back without moving his arm and before the amazement ever reached his face I hooked him one under the chin and he bit the damn cigar right in half.

I tapped Marty. "Who is he, sugar?"

Before she could answer the bartender said, "Al Reese, mister. You bought trouble. He's important. This is his district."

I said, "Oh," and grabbed hold of Al Reese's shirt. "You know me, Reese?"

He tried to bring back the sneer when I slapped him. It was a nice, loud slap, but I had the heel of my hand in it and his knees jerked.

"I asked you something."

This time he nodded.

"Say it loud, fat man. Let everybody hear you."

"Lieutenant Scanlon."

"Louder."

It came out louder and hoarser.

"You know what I think of slobs like you?"

I was getting the hand ready when he nodded again.

"Anybody pulls any crap on me like this again and I'll

26

brown you all out. I come from this place. I know the rules. When I don't like 'em I make up new ones. Maybe you played with some of the easy boys too long. Don't try it with me."

I let him go and he staggered away, clutching his hand against his chest. Both sides of our spot at the bar were empty now. Down the other end one guy in a grey suit was watching with amused, knowing eyes. Loefert, from the uptown mob.

Marty took a small sip of beer and touched her mouth nervously. "That was rough, Joe."

"You've seen it before, kid."

"But now you're *department*."

I grunted and picked up my brew. "Lesson one. Don't be afraid of letting them know who you are. They move first . . . then you move, only do it harder. Once these pigs get the bull on you, neither the department, nor the uniform, nor the gun is any good."

"But. . . "

"We're not in happy town, kid. This isn't a cross section of normal middle class morality."

"I live here, Joe. So do . . . did you."

"Sure, and now for lesson two. We're on a job and you're in the department too so stop moralizing."

For a moment she stiffened, then when she saw me laughing at her in the mirror she smiled back. "I've been in juvenile too long."

"I know. You've had to be nice to everybody. You've forgotten your heritage here though. In these parts it's the tough guy who has all the friends. Remember?"

"Too well."

"Come on, finish your beer and let's go up to your place. The icebox full?"

"It's a refrigerator, and yes it's full."

"Then let's go make like a romantic couple should."

Her eyes brightened mischievously. "What'll we do?"

"Eat, of course," I said. "Hell, we're cops, aren't we?"

CHAPTER THREE

I STOOD by the window thinking of my own comfortable bachelor quarters overlooking the Drive. The sun's passage over the canyon of the street had been brief, and now it lay in deepening shadows.

Behind me, Marty put the last of our notes away and poured from the fresh pot of coffee. She handed it to me silently, then watched the scene with me for a while.

"Thinking it's pretty terrible?" she asked.

"No. Just that it's three dimensional. From here the city is sight, sound and smell."

She shrugged and nodded. "But it's home."

"I prefer it a little more antiseptic."

"You're an old man and set in your ways."

I looked at her with the coffee halfway to my mouth. "Like hell!"

"Oh?" Those wild Irish eyes of hers went up and down me intently. "Most bachelors are out sowing. Not you. A fancy apartment, your own car and money in the bank. Duty comes first. For fun you take on extra assignments."

"How did . . ."

"I asked around, old buddy. Your friends told me."

"So?"

"So you're an old man and set in your ways. No real fun. No broads."

"Listen, I got broads. I got . . ."

"You got mad," she laughed.

Then I stopped and laughed too. "Well, like I said, it's been pretty antiseptic. The things I wanted on a cop's salary you have to make the hard way. You can do it easy too, but that puts you in another class I'm not interested in."

"They told me you were offered some fancy jobs."

"Unfortunately, then I just plain wanted to be a cop."

"Police officer."

"Police officer hell," I said. "That's for the upper etch bugheads who hate honesty. I like to be called a cop. You know why? Because that's what I am. Somebody yells, what do they yell? 'Call the cops' they yell. Not 'call a police officer.' You know what I am to those snot-nosed JD's? I'm a cop, that's what. Damn it, a *police officer* wouldn't last ten minutes outside Traffic Division with that tag."

"Okay, copper, okay. So I'm sorry. You ought to see your face, it's all screwed up red and tight and if I wasn't a broad you'd cream me, huh?" Her laugh was deep and throaty again and took all the annoyance away. I shook my head because I let her get me all riled up and turned and stared out the window again. Old Giggie. Jeepers. She put her coffee down and walked away.

On the street half a dozen kids fought for stickball rights in the middle of the road. They hung up two cars, but the drivers were too intent in the fight to bother blowing their horns. It ended quickly as they always do, then the cars crawled by and the game started.

Marta came out of the bedroom then. The grey tailored suit was gone and now she was in a sheer green thing that seemed to shimmer in the light, and what she did to her hair changed her face somehow and I had to wonder where all the beauty came from. She was full and proud in the breasts, with a casual way of standing with one leg partly thrust out that accentuated the incredible curve of her hips. Like that, the fabric of the dress ran flat across her belly, yet made you aware of other hidden curves still more lovely.

"You like?" she asked.

"I like," I said. "What's it for?"

"To give you a good reason for being here."

"It was good enough before," I grinned.

She walked closer, swirled around so I could see the overall effect. "But better now, huh?"

I nodded. "Better now." Then I grabbed her and pulled her close so I could smell the sweet scent in her hair and she was warm and hard against me, her fingers biting into my arm. Her mouth touched my mouth, warm and moist, the tip of her tongue soft and searching, saying hello after such a long, long time, a gentle touch because we were still new, even though very old.

I held her away and she smiled. "Nutty, isn't it?"

"Yeah. I'm not sure I understand it."

"Like this is nice work," she grinned.

I said, "On the job training."

She gave me that throaty laugh again, touched my lips with her finger and reached for her purse. She said, "We ready?"

I looked at my watch. It was a quarter to six and there was no time like the present. I nodded and said, "Let's go."

*　*　*

We picked Tony's Pizza for supper because René Mills had made it his special eatery. Nothing fancy about it, but Tony would put anybody from the neighborhood on the cuff. The old man remembered me with a black-faced nod not intended to be personal, but prohibition raids had long ago soured him on any kind of cop.

Fat Mary came over beaming and smiling, then patted me on the head like she used to do when she gave me a slice of hot Italian bread, thick with butter, for running errands for her.

When the sausage and peppers came Mary dished it up

29

herself and sat down opposite me, nodding with satisfaction as we ate. She liked to see people eat.

She said, "Now, Joe, you come back to see thees nice girl, no?" She didn't let me answer. "That is good. Very good. Long time thees nice girl should be marry. How to have the babies without the marry, no?"

"Well . . ."

She waggled a fat finger at me. "No. You marry first! Like I tell . . ."

But Tony broke it off. "Like you tell nobody. You let them eat, okay?"

Mary laughed so that her chins jiggled, then she reached over and patted my hand. "You a good boy, Joe. Now, how about rest of your family, eh? That crazy brother of yours still around?"

"I haven't seen him in a long while, Mary."

"Oh, he a funny one. Remember when he make believe he hang that kid and I scream and fall down the steps?"

Marta looked at me, puzzled. "The Davis kid," I explained. "They made this harness to go under his clothes, but it looked like he really was hung."

"Oh."

Mary's face drew into a stern grimace. "Not so funny yet. On the back I am all black and blue. Good thing I am there to see."

"Why?"

"Thees things they made to hold him up. One broke and he really was hanging." She shuddered. "For minute his face get red, his tongue come out. I take him down and I give that brother of yours one hell of a sock. Make his nose bleed. I was going to tell your papa, but he cry so I say nothing."

"First time I heard about that part of it."

"What was his name, what you called him? Something Indian."

"Chief Crazy Horse. A Sioux, I think. Big war leader under Sitting Bull."

"Oh, I tell you plenty things from them days."

Behind the bar Tony said, "Yak, yak. You let them eat, woman."

I winked at the old man and he scowled back friendly-like. Mary looked hurt, so I said casually, "See where René Mills died."

"No die." She hunched her heavy shoulders in a shrug. "He was killed."

"Yeah. Shot. Lots of that going on around here."

"Always trouble, Joe. You know that."

"René making it big here?"

She understood me, but waited a long moment before acknowledging it. "Not so big like he talked always. Big shot, that guy. Always talking about them . . . them *shooters*. His friends. Huh!"

"He always had a big mouth," I said. "Who'd he say his buddies were?"

Her typical Italian gesture was eloquent. "Who cares? Tough guys he likes. Always somebody in the papers who got trouble is his pal."

"He didn't have any loot around when he died."

"Always broke, that one. He pays his bills. Sometime take a month, but he come across."

"You're lucky," I said.

"What the cops do about it, eh, Joe?"

It was my turn to shrug. "He's on the books. Something'll turn up."

Her wise black eyes looked into me. "Like you maybe?"

I put down my fork. "Mary, I'm brass. I'm a lieutenant. You think I'm going to do legwork in this part of town?"

"So?"

"So let 'em shoot each other up all they want to. I'm going to make a pass at this mouse here and try to snag her out of this place."

Mary said, "Some mouse," and Marta jabbed me with her fork under the table. "Joe, no foolin'. You gonna do somethin' 'bout René?"

"What for?"

"You cop. We pay taxes and . . ." From behind the bar Tony growled in his usual way. Mary gave him a dirty look.

I said, "The cops were here and asked all the questions, weren't they?"

"Sure. They come. They ask. We tell. But what? Who knows from what, Joe? From a kid, like you, I know that one. He's what they call a sharpie. So what else?"

"Nothing else. What else is there?"

She drummed her fingers on the table top and pursed her mouth in thought. Then her finger went up dramatically. "Wait. I think of something." With a practiced motion she squeezed her bulk out of the seat and walked across the room with that peculiar lightness you sometimes see in fat people. A hurried talk in Italian with Tony got her yelled at, but she yelled back, then Tony rummaged around some papers beside his cash register and handed them to her. When she came back she laid them down and spread them open.

Marta and I looked at each other briefly. Mary said, "He left them here couple of nights before he get killed."

One was a four-color brochure on new model Caddies. The

other was the same, but for the Chrysler and it was folded back to the page showing the luxurious Imperial.

Mary was looking at me with raised eyebrows, waiting. I said, "He sure was thinking big, that's for sure."

She nodded. "This night he leave thees things, he pay his bill."

"How much?"

"T'ree hundred fifty somethin'."

"That's pretty steep to go, isn't it?"

"You know Tony," she said. "Most of that thees René drink. Tony, he buy him plenty booze and bring it to his room just before that."

"Oh?" I didn't want to push her.

"Tells me bunch of guys up there. They don't let him in. Just take the stuff and tell him pay later. You know Tony."

"So they were playing cards maybe," I said.

"Sure, maybe," she said and all her curiosity left.

I paid the bill, said so-long to Mary and Tony and took Marta out of there. She was all primed for a big talk, but inside, couldn't say anything that might have official sounding overtones. Now she wanted to talk and I wouldn't tell her anything. I just walked beside her grinning to see how much she could take.

We hit a couple of bars then, saying hello here and there, finding some of the old bunch still around. I made no bones about being a cop, but by then the news had preceded us anyway so it didn't make much difference. But one look at Marta and they knew I had a good reason to be around without wanting to get involved in police work. The winks were big and broad and I accepted them with a wink back.

It was a great cover. She spiked me with her damn heels a few times for pulling that stuff, but it was still real great cover.

At eleven-thirty I took her home, closed the door behind us and ducked the backhand she threw at me. I said, "You're supposed to use Judo."

"Oh, Joe!" But she had to smile. "I'm never going to ever be able to hold my head up around here any more."

"Why? You knew all those people."

"But I'm not a saloon jumper. Golly . . ."

"So we'll teach the old dog new tricks." This time the backhand got me before I could move out of reach.

Marta laughed, shook her head and said, "I'll go make coffee and you can tell me how we're doing. That is, if I'm allowed to know."

I said okay and sat down.

"Now tell me," she said.

"Not tell, sugar. Speculate. All we did was get seen around. All we speculate on is René Mills. Apparently he had some loot or was expecting some."

"He always looked the part. I never saw him in anything other than the latest styles."

"Sure," I agreed, "and he paid his bills. Those guys could always go that far rolling drunks. What gets me were those auto ads. Who needs a car around here? The kids would make a playground out of it in one day. Taxis and subways are too easy."

"He could have been just looking."

"Those folders were worn. He did a whole lot of looking."

"Somebody else could have had them first."

"Uh-huh," I agreed, "so we find out."

It took ten minutes. With a half a dozen calls I found the Caddie and the Imperial dealer who remembered Mills.

Marta said, "Well?"

"He did the asking himself. He sounded serious."

"René had something going for him then." She walked over with coffee and a plate of Danish and held them out.

"Who knows? He could still be playing the big shot."

We finished the snack and I looked at my watch. It was a quarter after twelve and I was beginning to drag. I got up, stretched and reached for my hat. Marta said, "Joe . . . it's been fun, really."

I grinned at her. "Work isn't supposed to be fun."

Her eyebrows went up. "You unhappy?"

"No. Come here." She came into my arms with a smile and a soft little sound and a way of doing it that was as if we had been doing it all our lives. We seemed to touch all over at once, then when the hot fire of her mouth engulfed mine, the touch became a demanding, writhing pressure and when I pushed her away she shuddered briefly, then opened her eyes.

"Little Giggie," I said.

"Big Giggie," she reminded me. "Don't do me like that or you'll get bitten."

"Never bite your superior officer," I said.

"Then watch yourself," she smiled. "Tomorrow?"

"In the afternoon. I have to go downtown first."

"You know you're leaving me in an awful mess," she said with a sultry grimace. Then she looked at me and grinned broadly when I stepped back.

I opened the door. "That makes two of us," I said.

On the way to the corner I saw Benny Loefert across the street talking to some chippy. I walked over and they stopped talking while I was still in the middle of the street. I said, "Turn around and put your hands against the wall, punk. You know the pose."

The arrogance in his eyes turned to little snakes of hate and he spit, then turned slowly. I made it faster with a shove of my hand. A handful of up-laters stopped to watch and you could hear the whispers and sense the heads in darkened windows of the tenements.

I patted him down to his shoes, made him show his identification then gave him at ease. He said, "What's that for? You know I don't go loaded."

"Ex-cons still in the punk business are always suspicious characters, punk. What're you doing here?"

"I got a broad."

"Who?"

He waved his thumb at the gum chewer and her eyes darted back and forth between us. "Let's see you shake her down, copper."

"Sure." But first I slapped him one across the mouth then gave him another across the ear. "That's for the smart mouth, punk. Try it again."

Some of the people watching grumbled, but just as many laughed. They didn't like punks either. I turned to the broad and pointed to the purse in her hand. "Get it out, kid, let's see it all. Who you are, where you live, the works."

"Listen . . . !"

"You ever do time, kid?"

Her eyes said yes. Her eyes said they didn't want to do any more, either. She opened the purse and showed me her Social Security card that gave her name as Paula Lees and a receipted bill for a room a block over. I knew what she was and the business she was in but didn't push it at all. When I told her okay and to put it away her eyes said thanks and gave Loefert a dirty look.

By tomorrow everybody would have the story. Loefert was part of big time moving downtown, but they weren't snot nosing this badge. When I moved them on I stood there a minute, said to hell with the subway and grabbed a cab cruising by.

It only took fifteen minutes to change the sight and sound and smells. I opened the door of my apartment and it was like being in a different world.

CHAPTER FOUR

AFTER breakfast in the cafeteria near headquarters, I went up to my desk and started clearing out details that had been laying over. In a way it was good to be on a single assignment. You had a chance to shove unfinished business on somebody else for a change, and for once you could devote yourself to thinking along a straight line.

Close to noon Mack Brissom gave his usual rap and opened the door. He had two containers of coffee, put them on the desk and settled down with a tired sigh.

I said, "What're you doing in on Sunday?"

"That Canadian business. It's in Homicide now."

I frowned, shook my head, but couldn't remember it.

"That armored car stickup in Montreal. One and half million."

"Why have we got it?"

Mack grunted and reached for his coffee. "Not *we*. Me. You're the fair-haired boy who don't have to work. The two guards are dead. Both the hoods who hit the truck were tracked to the Falls, crossed over into Buffalo and are supposedly heading toward New York."

"So catch 'em. You know who they are?"

"We know one. Charlie Darpsey. Used to be with the Brooklyn crowd. One of the guards was an ex-cop with a retirement job and recognized him from police fliers some years back. He lived long enough to pass out the name."

"Work, slob," I grinned.

He tipped the container up, swallowed noisily, then put it back. "Like you?" He was holding a smile back.

"What?"

"I happened to be in the Inspector's office earlier. Seems like you touched the wrong funny bone somewhere. The squawk was loud."

"It didn't reach me."

"For a while, I don't think it will. They're waiting to see if that kind of action gets any results." He leaned back and felt for a smoke in his pocket. He was out and looked at me disgustedly a second because I couldn't help him any. Then: "How's it going?"

"Nothing yet, you know how it goes. I saw Benny Loefert around there."

Mack nodded. "That's what I came in to tell you about. A couple of pigeons reported in that Loefert, Beamish, Will Fater and Steve Lutz have been moving around."

"High-priced guns?"

"Yeah. All but Lutz took rooms in the area. They're giving the place real class."

"I shook Loefert down last night. Gave him a little bang to set him straight."

"We heard about that too. Beat cop picked it up. You meet him yet?"

"No."

"Nice kid. Just off probationary duty. Turns in reports like they'll be kept for posterity. Detailed? Hell, he'd even turn in the number of spit marks on the sidewalk if he thought it necessary."

"He'll make out. We were all like that," I said.

"Sure." He got up and picked his container off the desk. "We're going to keep track of the uptown lads. If anything comes through we'll pass it along."

"Right. And thanks for the coffee."

He winked and left. I finished filing the papers, marked them for proper distribution and called for Cassidy to take care of them. Then I phoned Marta and told her I'd be over about two and to have lunch ready. She called me a house-maid-hugging flatfoot and hung up.

Sunday on the street was a day of truce. The week had been fought to a smashing climax on Saturday night and now the troops had withdrawn and cleared the field for a little while. But the signs of battle were still there, the bright flakes of broken bottles, the vomit splashes by the walls, a garbage can on its side in the curb.

Traffic was negligible, but the kids had that uneasy Sunday feeling that couldn't make up into a stickball game. The young girls were out, purses swinging, jaws chewing, taking this one day to prove their respectability while their opposites tried hard for masculine worldliness with smelly vestibules and dirty stoops for a background. None of it came off. It was still a battlefield.

The bars had opened at one and so far were almost empty. The three I stopped in had just been mopped down and smelled of furniture polish. *The hell with the house, but take care of that bar!* In each place I asked if Al Reese had been in, and when they said no I told them to pass the word I was looking for him and was going to beat the crap out of him when I found him. I did him a little dirty by hinting that he was a stoolie of sorts, and in that neighborhood even a rumor like that can get a guy in pretty deep water.

But at least they were taking it right. I was the tough cop who came back to the street where he used to live to see a broad he grew up with. So long as everybody stayed in line, what they did was no business of mine. None at all. Anybody plays it wise, they get rapped and I could make it stick. They were getting to know that part in a hurry. That's the way they had it figured, and that's just what we wanted them to think.

At five minutes of two Marta opened the door for me and I could smell lunch on the table. This time she had on a dress with a billowy skirt and regular whore shoes. Only on her the combination looked great.

We ate without saying much, went out to a crummy movie house and saw a picture we had both seen a year ago. At seven we had supper at Smith's Bar and Grill, then went back to the neighborhood for a few beers before calling it a night.

Two days and the pattern was working out. The word ran like a swift river in those parts and wherever we stopped conversation stopped too. Words were guarded and eyes could evade mine for no reason except I was cop. On the street the lushes and the panhandlers would throw a half-hearted ingratiating smile, then scurry away quickly.

On the way back to the apartment I saw the beat cop and crossed over to his side, holding Marta's arm. I had never seen him, but he knew who I was and touched his cap. "Evening, Lieutenant."

"Hi." I stuck out my hand and he took it. "Mack Brissom told me to look you up."

He flushed and grinned. "Didn't think he'd remember me. He was one of the instructors at the academy. By the way, I'm Hal McNeil."

"This is Marta Borlig."

He nodded. "I've seen you often, Miss Borlig."

I nudged her in the ribs, "See, like a sore thumb."

"Oh, pipe down," she said pleasantly.

"Quiet around the beat?" I asked him.

"Usual stuff. Last few days a mysterious prowler scared a couple of old ladies. Guy with a face full of whiskers. Big fight two blocks over a week ago and a running feud with three families involved ever since."

"Hard to handle?"

He shrugged and said seriously, "Nothing the rule book can't cope with."

"Well, good to see you, McNeil. Keep an eye on my gal here, okay?"

"That's an easy job, sir," he chuckled back. He walked off

37

trying store fronts and nodding to upstairs residents. Good boy, that.

On the way to the apartment Marta stopped at the place I had avoided so long. She looked across the street to the blank face of the brick walls, then at me. "Does it hurt that much to look at it, Joe?"

The house I lived in, I thought, where hunger was a constant hazard that separated living into feasts and famines. Downstairs a guy had murdered his wife and kids while they slept and blew his own brains out afterwards. One floor up Bloody Mary started in business, first with abortions that got her the name, then to a three-bed shag joint until she made enough loot to move to the corner.

"It doesn't really hurt at all," I said.

"They'll be ripping them down in a few months. All three of those buildings were condemned."

"Twenty years too late," I said, still picturing half-forgotten faces that seemed to be perpetually leaning out of windows staring vacuously into the street, their arms propped on faded old pillows.

"You still hate it, don't you?"

I nodded. "I've always hated it. Not only the houses. This whole place. This dirty end of the city, the poverty, the squalor. Hardly a chance to get out."

"You got out."

I said, *"Hardly.* Besides, I hated it enough." I looked at the indifference on her face. "I can't see how you stood it."

"Maybe I couldn't hate anything that much. Come on, take me home. Tomorrow's another day."

"Sure. Let's go."

I said so long in the vestibule, quick, because I didn't feel like talking to anyone nice. The old house had turned me inside out again, and right now all I wanted was something to wash the taste out. I walked back to Donavan's Dive, went in and got a beer. In the back something big and fat made a hurried exit through the family exit, and I felt a little better.

When I finished the second the little guy who had been watching me so intently finally caught my eye and I knew what he meant. When I left I headed west, halted in the shadow of a doorway and waited. Five minutes later the little guy came by and when I said, *"Here,"* he ducked in beside me.

CHAPTER FIVE

"You're Scanlon . . . Lieutenant Scanlon, right?" It was a statement rather than a question.

"Read off your dog tags, mister," I told him.

Nervously, he poked his head out and peered down each direction before huddling back in the shadows, "Harry Wope. I got a flop upstairs over Moe Clausist's hock shop. Work around some, but mostly it's Social Security."

"Done time?"

"Six weeks on a vag charge ten years ago." He shrugged and added, "It was a bad year. Look, you won't say nothin' about . . ."

"Don't sweat it, Harry. What do you want?"

"That fat slob Reese is after your can, Mr. Scanlon. He got the word in and . . ."

"I've heard it."

"Hell, I don't mean downtown only like city hall. He's lookin' for somebody to hand you lumps. Trouble is, he can't find nobody, but if he keeps lookin' he sure will. He'll blow five hundred to see you dragged out of an alley."

"Where did you pick this one up?"

"Big ears. I was dumpin' garbage for Hilo when he was on the phone inside. One of the windows is broke and I heard him."

I said, "I'm not handing out favors, Harry. Why put me wise?"

Harry Wope leaned toward me, his wrinkled face turned up toward mine, his eyes squinting at me. "You don't remember me, do you? Nope, guess you wouldn't at that. No reason to after all. Me and your father was in France together during the First World War. He saved my ass once. I used to come around when you was a kid. He only had four then when I seen you last. Knew your ma too."

Then I remembered him. A funny guy who wore his uniform until there was nothing left of it, having Saturday breakfasts in our kitchen and eating like a wolf to make up for a week of missed meals. "Thanks, Harry. I'll remember it."

"If I hear anything more, I'll let you know."

"Don't stick your neck out," I said.

* * *

I toured the area slowly, letting the familiar things reestablish themselves. On the side of Carmine's grocery I ran my hand over the deeply carved initials Larry and I had put there with Doug Kitchen's and René Mills' underneath. A dozen layers of paint had not been enough to fill them in. At the school yard where Noisy Stuccio and Hymie Shapiro had sat in the cab of the rubbish truck and accidentally knocked it into gear the long gash still showed in the brick wall.

All dead now, I thought. We had all scrambled over rooftops together, saved empty deposit bottles for Saturday movies, reenacted those same pictures in the park, turning from cowboys and Indians into soldiers or cops and robbers, depending on what had played. Maybe the pattern had started then. Larry ate up the Indian roles. He even had a headdress and a tomahawk. At nine I was the cop. Noisy, Hymie and René went the George Raft route and fancied themselves hotshot mobsters. Doug Kitchen wanted to be a sailor, only they hardly ever had Navy movies unless they were musical comedies, and Doug felt like he had two left feet all the time.

And Marta . . . little Giggie . . . trailed us around throwing rocks at us because she was a girl and didn't belong in the game. I grinned and felt the tiny scar at my hairline where she connected one time. She got a boot in the tail for that one and ran home bawling.

It was one-thirty when I turned the corner and walked toward the spot where Doug Kitchen had died. Down farther, across the street, a pair of drunks argued noisily about nothing; on the stoops here and there couples huddled in the darkness, taking advantage of the only time there was any privacy at all. A few loud voices bellowed from behind closed windows in the upper apartments, sounds that never seemed to change in volume or subject matter. On my side, coming toward me, a late-shift worker ambled along watching his feel until another person stepped out of the shadows, said something that made him hesitate a few seconds before he kept walking, while the other one went back into the shadows.

He passed me without anything more than a glance while I kept walking to where he had the contact, and when I reached there the girl stepped out of her spot beside the balustrade, handbag swinging, voice deliberately provocative, and said, "In a hurry, mister?"

"Nope."

"I could be company if you want to go somewhere."

"Sounds good," I said. "How much?"

I sensed her smile, and saw the way she thrust her body out to accentuate her breasts and hips. "Ten'll get you more than you have a right to expect."

"Deal, kid," I said. Then I took a cigarette out, stuck it between my lips and fired it up. When she saw my face her breath was sucked in so hard she nearly choked. "Hello, Paula," I said.

Paula Lees' face was a pale oval in the yellow light of the match. Her mouth started to quiver, and for a second I thought she was going to make a break for it so I reached out and took her arm. She shook her head and almost whispered, "Please . . ."

"You could take a fall, Paula. Soliciting . . . a vag rap. Maybe eighteen months in detention."

She caught the implication of that one word . . . *could.* "What . . . do you want, Mr. Scanlon?"

"Where's your place?"

Paula looked back over her shoulder. "Right here."

"Let's go inside then."

The tiny flat was typical of all the others around it, existing within a myriad of smells both human and vegetable. The walls were scratched and dirty, the paper peeling, the plaster cracked, and no attempt at rejuvenation could dent the squalor of the place.

Her apartment consisted of two rooms and a bathroom someone had made out of a closet, a combination living room and kitchen with an adjoining bedroom. Paula didn't get the picture straight. She headed for the bedroom immediately and started to undress. She had her blouse and bra off and the zipper down on her skirt when I said, "Put them back on, kid."

She jerked her head around. "But . . ."

I didn't let her finish. "I'm not taking a pay-off in trade."

Fractured modesty suddenly overcame her then. She edged behind the door and when she came out again she was dressed, spots of red showing high on her cheekbones and her mouth drawn into a tight, angry line. "I'm not doing any special tricks, Mr. Scanlon. None of that fancy stuff . . ."

"Sit down and shut up."

Paula spun around at my tone, licked her lips nervously and did as she was told. After a minute of staring at her shoes she looked up and said, "Well?"

"How many kids working this street, Paula?"

She thought about it, shrugged and said, "Just me. It ain't too good here."

"Why stay?"

41

Her eyes seemed to crawl to mine. "Because *they* won't let me go nowhere else." I didn't say anything. I just sat there. She added, "When Bummy Lentz and Loefert came down I scratched Bummy up and told Loefert off. Now they don't let me off this block, the bastards."

"Still the same old routine, isn't it? Hoods still pushing the hustler trade. Where does Loefert come in?"

Paula shook her head. "He didn't do nothing but make a call to the right guy."

"Al Reese?"

She didn't answer. She didn't have to.

I grinned. "Bummy won't bother you any more. He got tanked on some bad booze with a wood alcohol base two weeks ago and died in Bellevue."

"So the call still goes."

"Maybe," I said. "I'll get the heat off you, but you get the hell off this street and find a job. There's enough work in this town without wearing your tail out."

"And for this you want what?" she challenged.

I said, "You've been out there every night, haven't you?"

Paula nodded.

"Your name didn't show as a witness to Doug Kitchen's death." When she looked down at her feet again I knew I had her. Like everybody else, she had been interviewed by the Homicide team but gave a negative answer. "You saw it, didn't you?"

She knew what would happen if she tried to lie out of it. She'd sweat it out downtown with a soliciting charge over her head. Silently, she nodded again.

"Let's hear it, kid."

For a few seconds she sat there, then glanced up resignedly and said, "I saw him coming down the block, all right. Hell, I didn't know it was him. He stopped and waved to somebody across the street who was going by under the light, but it was too far for me to see who it was. I saw him start to cross over and so did the other guy, then Doug sort of stopped, talked a little bit and began to back up. All of a sudden he started to run and this other guy, he just shot him right in the back. When Doug didn't fall he shot twice again, and he fell right on the sidewalk. That other guy . . . he just walked away up the street."

"What did you do?"

"Do? I went back inside, that's what I did. I didn't come out until the next morning. And I told a john I was going see him that night too."

"Anything recognizable about the other guy?"

Paula shook her head. "It was too far away."

"Think some more, Paula. A kill always has something special about it. Once you see it happen you don't forget it very easily."

Tight lines appeared at the corners of her eyes and she suddenly looked older than she was. "Honest, Mr. Scanlon . . ." She paused, bit her lip, then said, "It ain't nothing, but that other guy . . . he let out a yell like."

"What kind of yell?"

"Just a funny yell, then he shot him and walked away. It wasn't loud, but I heard him. There wasn't traffic or nothing right then. I heard him yell, that's all. It didn't sound right. I was scared. Honest, Mr. Scanlon . . ."

"Forget it, Paula." I got up from the chair and slapped on my hat.

"What are you going to . . . do with me?"

"Not a thing, kid. Vice isn't my specialty. I'm not here on a case. It's just that I knew Doug Kitchen when we were all living around here. As far as you're concerned, I'll do what I said I'd do. If you're smart you'll get your tail off this street too."

She believed me then and something changed in her eyes. "Gee," she told me, "it's hard to believe a cop would . . . well . . ." Paula lowered her eyes demurely, then caught mine again. Briefly, she glanced toward the bedroom. "If you'd like . . . I could show you . . . like real special things and . . ."

"Uh-uh," I said. "I got all I can handle right now," I lied. But she didn't know it and smiled as if she did.

* * *

The reports had listed only one other witness who wasn't sure of what he had seen at all, a drunk coming out of a stupor he had laid on all day, who had seen the kill from the stairway going into the cellar at number 1209. The first shot made him look up and on the next he had seen Doug fall. Then he ducked down below the cement wall and stayed there. He thought he remembered a guy standing in the street but couldn't be sure and he wasn't the kind of witness you bothered pressing. If anybody else saw the incident he wasn't talking. Right now the department had their own stoolies asking around, but in that neighborhood there was a natural, inborn reluctance to even mention anything that would make any more trouble than was already there, so it was doubtful if anything would turn up.

Walking back I reviewed what the sheets had stated. René Mills was found dead behind a building and only one person

43

had mentioned hearing what could have been a gunshot and wasn't sure of the time. Hymie Shapiro was killed inside his car where it was parked outside his apartment. Noisy Stuccio was shot in the tenement where he lived with the TV turned on full and if the sound hadn't been up so high that the guy downstairs came up to complain, the body wouldn't have been found for days.

Somebody was doing it nice and neatly. Very pro.

And there was one thing I was sure of. It wasn't over yet. Interwoven in the wild hodgepodge of murders there was a peculiar pattern. So far the theme of it hadn't emerged yet, but it would. It would. It was just too bad that somebody else would have to die before it showed all the way.

When it did I'd be there and a killer would be under the end of my gun with the big choice of dying on the spot or sweating it out in a mahogany and metal chair with electrodes on his legs and one on his head that was the big, permanent nightcap.

There was one more stop I wanted to make before the night was over. I walked one block, turned the corner and went in the vestibule beside Trent's candy store and struck a match to look at the nameplate over the bells on the wall. A tarnished copper strip read R. CALLAHAN and I nudged the button. A minute later the automatic trip clicked on the door and I pushed it open, went up the stairs to the landing and waited outside the door.

Fifteen years ago Ralph Callahan had been retired from the force, but he had spent his life on the beat in his own neighborhood and you could never take the department out of the man. His eyes would still see, his mind classify events with practiced skill, even though he wasn't active, but like every other retired police officer, he still had certain privileges extended him by the city including carrying a badge and a gun if he chose to.

When he opened the door he made me with a glance, nodded curtly and said, "Come on in, son."

"Hello, Ralph." He was a big guy even yet, filling out his pajamas in a stance that marked thousands of days in a uniform.

He waved me to a kitchen chair after closing the bedroom door softly. "The missus is a light sleeper," he told me and sat down on the other side of the table. "Now . . . don't remember you, but you look familiar." I started to reach for my badge, but he waved me off. "I know *what* you are all right, son."

44

I grinned at him. "Joe Scanlon. You laid a couple across my behind with that stick of yours when I was a kid."

"Well, I'll be damned," he said. "Now where are you?"

"Homicide. Special detail right now. Marta Borlig's working it with me."

"Damn, ain't the department getting tricky?" He studied me a few seconds, then leaned forward on the table, his hands folded together. "Those four kills?"

"Uh-huh. Smell anything?"

"If I did I would have reported it. Nobody knows a thing."

His eyes watched me shrewdly, and I said, "There's another interesting angle."

"That's what I was waiting for you to say. Loefert and the others showing up?"

"That's right," I agreed. "What does it look like to you?"

"They're out of place around here, that's what it looks like. The only rackets going on are small stuff. Numbers, a few books . . . that sort of thing. A few hustlers work around, but it's all normal procedure, and not big enough to crack down on. Hell, nobody's got enough money in this neighborhood to lay on hard."

"But they're here, so it must mean something else."

The elderly cop leaned back and frowned at the ceiling. "I got an idea that could connect."

"Oh?"

He lowered his eyes and steadied them on mine. "Remember that guy . . . Gus Wilder, the one who jumped bail in Toledo when he was going to testify against the Gordon-Carbito mob?"

"I saw the flyers and read the news accounts."

Ralph bobbed his head. "He lived two blocks over for five years. Still got a brother there. The brother's straight . . . runs a dry cleaning shop, but I'm thinking they're watching him to see if Wilder makes a contact."

"Why?"

Callahan grinned at me. "Things you brass cops seem to forget. The Gordon-Carbito mob upstate did the local boys a favor once . . . a big one. Could be now the locals are returning it by keeping an eye out for Wilder. If he talks the upstate combo will fall."

"A possibility," I agreed. I stood up and pushed the chair back. "Keep your ears open . . . I'll appreciate it. If you need a contact, try Marta Borlig, only keep it on the q.t. that she's on the force."

"Will do, Joe."

"Thanks for your time."

"Don't mention it."

I said good night and went downstairs to look for a cruising cab.

* * *

My morning reports were finished at nine and I handed them to Mack Brissom. "Want some coffee? I'm meeting Marty at the diner."

"Can't do, friend. I'm tied up with that Montreal thing. A cross check on the ballistics came in and the gun used in Montreal was the same used in an attempted bank heist in Windsor a week earlier and to kill a gas station attendant in Utica four days after the Montreal bit."

"That's not our jurisdiction," I said.

"Yeah, I know. But the gun was found in a B.M.T. subway train by a passenger and turned in. No prints, unregistered and probably deliberately left there. It could be a red herring dodge to keep the action here while the killer is miles away, but we have to push it all the way."

"Any of the money showing up yet?"

"Nothing. Lousy thing is, who could tell? Only part of the loot was in bills big enough to have the serial numbers recorded. It's like the Brinks job . . . they'll hold off until things quiet down before dumping the stuff."

"Well, have fun."

Mack didn't seem to hear me. He shook his head, looking out the window. "Screwy deal, that one. The bank heist was a bust because four detectives were on the premises cashing their checks and stopped it. The Montreal job took a lot of planning . . . more than one single week. That was a top operation."

"Maybe the guy who used the gun was brought in just to give them cover," I suggested.

"Ah, I don't know. It smells. It's real sour. We got a tipoff from Canada that something had been in the wind a long time. Two mobsters from the States had been spotted up there a couple months earlier and sent back across the line, *persona non grata*. The day after the job an abandoned American automobile was found three miles from the scene that had been stolen in Detroit a week before, so there's a general tie-in.

"Take the guy with the gun . . . he grabbed a car in Detroit, ran over to Windsor to pull the bank job, muffed it, then pulled the Montreal deal, dumped the car and took off. A report from a motel in the area where the car was left, that catered to tourists from the States, called in a stolen car with Jersey plates the same day."

I said, "It looks nice except for that one thing, Mack. You don't plan that kind of holdup in a week . . . not on the run, anyway."

Mack collected his papers from the desk and folded them under his arm as one of the duty officers came in and handed him a sheet. He looked at it, scowled, then glanced at me. "That stolen car from Jersey was found in the Bronx."

"The boy's coming home," I grinned.

"So he takes the subway, leaves the gun there so he can't get picked up with it and finds a hideout. But where?"

"Why don't you try the Ritz," I suggested. "He'd have enough cash along to afford the rates."

"Drop dead."

We left together and I went down to meet Marty at the diner. She was already there, tall, fresh and cool looking in a trim suit that couldn't hide her loveliness no matter how businesslike it was cut. She had coffee and pie ready for me and a notepad open on the table in front of her. I said, "Hi, little Giggie," and sat down.

"If you weren't my superior you'd hear something," she told me.

"Superior in all things, sugar."

"All?"

"Like I said . . . all."

"Maybe you need a lesson, big boy."

"In what?" I grinned.

"Oh, shut up." She sipped at her coffee, then pulled the pad toward her. "I had a talk with a few people on the block."

"And . . . ?"

"Remember what Fat Mary said about René Mills hinting about coming into some money?"

"Uh-huh."

"Confirmed. He was seen with a roll, paid off two big bar bills, cleaned up an account overdue by three months at the grocer's and made a pitch at Helen Gentry who has pretty expensive tastes and only goes with the boys who are loaded. On top, he laid in a case of expensive Scotch whiskey and paid for it in cash."

"So?"

Marty closed the pad and said, "He'd been pimping for those two girls who live over Papa Jones' store for three years now. Cheap trade, and the take couldn't have been big, but it was all he had, then suddenly he tells them both to take off . . . that he's going out of business."

"Not much cash was found on the body," I said. "None of that Scotch was found in the apartment, either."

"Screwy," she mused.

I told her about my conversation with Ralph Callahan the night before and she nodded, thinking the same thing I was. I said, "He could have been hiding out Gus Wilder for a price."

"We could check and see if they ever had a previous contact."

"Not now we can't, kid. You're supposed to be a working girl. Until tonight we'll go at it from a different angle. If the local mob is looking for Wilder they'll have their own sources. Let's see if they really are. Think you can run a check?"

"Sure. Regulation procedure accelerated by native ingenuity. I'll see those who are assigned to that detail."

I finished my coffee and dropped a bill on the table. "Good enough. I'll pick you up at the apartment tonight." I started to leave, then stopped and turned around. "Don't get involved personally. Let somebody else do the legwork."

"I can handle it myself, Joe."

"Perhaps, but I don't want you to lose your cover. Probe too far and some newshawk will get curious and your picture will be in the paper. That would wipe out your effectiveness in the neighborhood."

"All right, Joe," she smiled, "I'll be careful." But all that time she knew what I really meant. I was getting a damn funny feeling about that woman, one I had never experienced before. Something that was like a fist tightening in my belly and sending a warm, crawly sensation across my back.

CHAPTER SIX

HENRY WILDER'S dry cleaning place was a hole-in-the-wall operation that catered to the local trade. Enough business kept him from poverty, but he was never going to get rich there. He lived upstairs over his store, a prematurely balding bachelor about fifty with tired lines around his eyes and a nervous flutter to his hands. I caught him on his lunch hour, flashed my badge and got invited in to a shabby room cluttered with junk and three racks of clothes customers had either forgotten about or didn't have the money to redeem.

48

When I sat down he fidgeted on the edge of his chair waiting for me to speak. Finally I said, "Ever hear from your brother Gus?"

"That bum!"

"I didn't ask that."

"Sometimes I get a letter. He was up on charges in Toledo."

"Hear from him since?"

Henry Wilder was going to say no, but knew he couldn't make the lie stick. "Sure . . . a phone call. After he jumped bail."

"Where was he?"

He licked his mouth nervously and toyed with the food on his plate. "He ain't that simple. He called direct."

"Why?"

His eyebrows went up then. "Money. What else? He wants me to send him five hundred bucks. Now where the hell am I supposed to get five hundred bucks? He didn't even ask. He just told me to get it ready and he'd tell me where to send it."

"Going to?"

Once again, his tongue snaked out. "I . . . don't know." He took a sip of coffee to wet his mouth and added, "I'm scared of him. I always was."

"He's your brother, isn't he?"

Wilder shook his head. "Stepbrother. Hell, I'd sooner turn him in, only it might not work and he'd come after me." His eyes held a pleading expression. "What am I supposed to do?"

"The cops aren't the only ones looking for Gus, buddy."

"I know. That's what I figured. So I'm caught in the middle either way," he said.

"Then take a chance and play it right. If he calls you, call us. We have ways of keeping things quiet."

"Can . . . I think about it?"

"Sure. One way or another he'll turn up, but like you said, why get caught in the middle? He asked for anything he gets."

I went to get up, then changed my mind and asked, "You know the girls René Mills had working for him?"

For a second his face took on a startled look, then he nodded. "Rose Shaw and Kitty Muntz. They come in all the time. Rose should be in soon to pick up her stuff. That Mills, he gave 'em the boot before he kicked off."

"So supposing we go downstairs and wait for her, Henry."

"In the shop?" He swallowed hard, knowing what they thought of cops around here.

"Don't worry, I'll even help out behind the counter."

Rose Shaw didn't show until ten after three, a flagrant little whore with a hard, tight body encased in a too-small sweater and blouse combination, her eyes showing the cynicism of her profession, the caustic twist to her mouth accentuating it. She threw her ticket down on the counter top with a crumpled ten-dollar bill from a plastic purse and stood there with a hurry-up look on her face.

I got up from the stool where I was sitting while Henry Wilder was collecting her clothes. She made me as fast as Ralph Callahan did, but in a different way. The lids half closed over her pupils and the mouth went into a semi-sneer that spat *copper*, and she was ready to tell me to stuff it because she wasn't working a pad at the moment and there was nothing I could lay on her. She was too wise to get trapped by a phoney approach, and wasn't about to get stuck with a pay off if I was a bad one.

One by one the possibilities ran through her mind, eliminating the wrong ones, and when I still didn't make a move her face clouded because she couldn't tap the right answer. Then she got jumpy. There is something peculiar about those on the stiffer sides of the fence, the law and the punks. In some ways they seem to look alike sometimes. They work in the same areas in the same profession with the same people, and it gets to them so they adopt common mannerisms and expressions and deep in the back of their eyes is buried a mutual hatred for each other.

But we had the advantage. We could read them. They could never quite read us. They were the ones who were mixed up, not us.

I said, "Talk or walk, Rose."

"Look, mister . . ."

The badge lay in my hand, nicely palmed. "Talk here, walk downtown. Take your pick."

She said something under her breath and glanced around her. "Screw you, copper. Not in public."

"You name it then."

"I got a room at 4430. It's where I live, not work."

"Go ahead. I'll give you ten minutes."

"Second floor in the back." She swore under her breath, draped her clothes over her arm, picked up her change and walked out, her face still full of disgust.

I gave her the ten minutes and picked my way down to her brownstone, cut in quickly and shoved the door open. The odor of burned grease and cabbage was heavy on the air, cutting through the mustiness of dirt and decay. The steps were hollowed by the tread of thousands of feet traversing them, creaky with age and littered with odds and ends of callous living. I found her door, knocked once and turned the knob without being asked to come in.

Rose Shaw sat with her feet up on a table, a beer in her hand, deliberately posed so I could see up her dress past the muscular smoothness of her thighs. I said, "Forget the peep show, Rose," and swung a chair around and sat down with my arms lying across its back.

"Swing me, copper. I'm waiting to hear the pitch."

"Let's start with René Mills."

She shrugged elaborately and took a pull from the can of beer. "He's dead. What else?"

"Why, Rose?"

"I can think of a hundred reasons. Somebody beat me to it. Kitty too. Hell, she pulled out before René was knocked off. I thought she was dumber'n me, but she saw the signs, she did. She knew what was coming and cut out before she was told to."

"Where is she?"

"Jersey City. She left yesterday. Her old man let her go back to work for him in a factory. She won't like it."

"And how about you?"

"What the hell do you care?"

"I don't."

"So why the action?" she asked.

"René Mills," I repeated.

"You seem to know the score. Where do I come in? So I'm puttin' out for cash, man. It ain't the best, but it'll do until something better shows." She lost her hate for a second and stared at the ceiling. "Would you believe it, I used to be big time. Miami, then, and that was only four years ago. I was seventeen and rolling in the long green. Man, what days."

"What happened?"

"I got clapped up and handed it out, and like that I was out. Two trips to the medic and I was okay, but the curse was there, man. So what's new?"

"Get back to René Mills."

She made a face and finished the beer. "He took me on. Me and Kitty. We was broke, willing and able. The trade was lousy compared to the other, but that's the breaks. He set up the scene, we split fifty-fifty only we paid all the bills." She gave another of those resigned shrugs and said, "We made out."

"Why'd he drop you then?"

"Went big time . . . like ha ha. He always had ideas and they got him dead. So this time he tells us to get lost, lays on a hundred bucks apiece when he's all grins and new shoes

51

with that watch back on his wrist he stole from some guy in a bar and hocked . . . got eighty bucks for it from Norman at the hockshop, so it was worth plenty."

"How, Rose?"

"Who knows, copper? You think he'd spill? Hell, he booted Noisy Stuccio out of his pad a week before, and you know how close they were. Sure, old René had somethin' going for him all the way."

"And what would you say it was?"

She reached back over her shoulder, opened the small refrigerator and took out another bottle of beer. She didn't offer me one. When she jacked the top off she said, "It was fresh money he didn't expect. It came sudden like, but I'll tell you this . . . he couldn't get his hands on all of it. What he had was plenty, but not the large stuff. He liked to talk big, and kept hinting at what he was going to come into, but I knew that slob too damn well. He was thinking and working on something he didn't have but sure damn well expected to get one way or another. That bastard wouldn't let a penny get past him if he could help it."

"Who supplied it?"

"What's it get me, copper?" She eyed me curiously, waiting for my answer.

"Ask," I said.

She started to speak, stopped and gave me one more of those shrugs and went back to her beer.

"I can give you advice," I said.

"Screw your advice," she told me coldly. "No advice from a cop."

"I got a friend who makes pictures. We were in the war together. He might be able to use your type if you have the guts to try. Maybe it won't work, but I can always ask."

"Why?"

"Why not?"

I was starting to feel like a damn dogooder and didn't like it. Thirty days in the can would probably make more of an impression, but she was from the place I grew up and couldn't get out and I knew what she felt like.

Rose looked at me, the beer motionless in her hand. "You mean it, don't you?"

I nodded.

"What's this world coming to?" she said. "So I've tried everything, why not advice from a cop?" The hardness washed out of her eyes and the expression turned serious. "René had somebody stashed in his apartment. Somebody he knew."

"How did *you* know that?"

"Because he was buying groceries for two, that's why. I saw him at the deli, old Pops mentioned it and once I saw the laundry he brought into the laundromat. He bought booze he'd never buy for himself and he had those allover smiles he never had when times was hard."

"Who, Rose?"

"I never inquired. If I did it would mean a belt in the mouth and I had enough of that, and in my business that would be . . ."

"Disastrous," I supplied.

"Yeah."

I got up and pushed the chair back where it was. "I'll make that call for you. Take it."

"Okay, copper," she said. She lifted the bottle to her lips, sipped at it without taking her eyes from mine, then put it down and smiled. "And you know what? I'll make it, too." When I agreed with a little grin she said, "Watch out for that Al Reese. He had the bull on René and was pushing him. You're the copper I've been hearing about, aren't you?"

"Probably."

"Then watch him. He knew René had dough coming. I saw them arguing one day and it was all on Al's side. He had René pinned because of something he knew René did, like he does with everybody else, and held it over his head. When René started flashing that cabbage, Al was there, so he put things together and put the squeeze on him. Don't play that fat boy down, copper. He's just a precinct captain around here, but dig his place on the Sound and that boat he has and the broads he pays for and you'll see more. The tax people ought to do him like they did Capone. Where he lives here is only for show to get the votes for the party like he's one of the boys, but he's a power, man, a big power."

"I'll watch him," I said.

"He's smart."

"So am I."

"He's tough."

"I'm a helluva lot tougher, sugar."

"But he knows more about René and that's what you're interested in, isn't it?"

"You're on the ball."

"I like you, copper. You're welcome to stay a while if you want."

For fun I winked like maybe I'd be back, but we both knew what it meant. Twice now I'd been invited to a bed party free by a couple of pros who could make it interesting and twice I kissed off the deal. *Too much training, I thought. Too many Army VD films.*

53

Hell, that wasn't the reason. It was that damn Marty. I kept thinking about her.

* * *

The late-afternoon shift was just beginning to drift into Donavan's place when I got there. This was the straight bunch, the guys still in work clothes carrying lunch pails, having a drink before they had to breech the fortresses of their own homes. The bartender caught my entry and tried to pass the word, but I stopped him with a single look and went back to where Donavan was sitting behind a paper and pulled it away from his face.

"Al Reese," I said. "Where is he?"

His tone was bland, but forced. "He ain't been in."

All I had to do was start that damn vicious grin again.

"Try Bunny's," he said in a hurry. He covered his fright by looking at his watch. "He don't generally come over here until six."

I said, "You make a call, Donavan, you put the word out and I'll smear you all over your own joint. You got that?"

"Listen, Scanlon . . ."

Tough guys I didn't like. I just grinned again, and he got the message. Whatever he saw in my face scared the crap out of him. "Look . . . I got my own business . . ."

I didn't bother to hear him out.

Bunny's was a fag joint around the bend. Hell, you've probably read about it a dozen times if you keep up with the columns. At night a cop is stationed outside and a cruiser goes by every ten minutes looking for trouble. It was an old place and back when Prohibition was still in effect and the stage door Johnnies were still escorting the chorus babes around as status symbols and it was a genuine saloon, Larry and I were making bucks for eating money holding open car doors for the tux crowd and sometimes steering the lonelies to spots where exciting company could be found in a hurry.

Now it was changed, the exterior was gaudy, the canopy and doorman expensive, the line of taxis unusually long for this area at this time, but the reason plain . . . it was the convention season, and the out-of-towners wanted a peek at New York in the rough.

I could still feel Larry at my side, laughing at the suckers, knowing what marks they'd be when a forlorn lad was out for a favor and a broad watching to see how expansive her date would be. Hell, that was how he got his loot to go watch all the Tom Mix shows.

Chief Crazy Horse, I kept thinking. Miss you, boy. Of all

that big family we had, I miss you the most. One lousy war and a *missing in action* notification telegram busts us up.

You didn't miss a thing, Larry. The world went wild after you left. Most of the bunch are dead. Some died with you . . . some the hard way. Some are still waiting to die. The rest just waiting.

I went inside.

Al Reese was at the bar, his bulk taking up a corner of it. Loefert was two stools down with a pretty, but hard-looking B girl beside him, and next to her Will Fater and Steve Lutz were sipping drinks without talking, satisfied with watching their reflections in the back bar mirror.

It was going to be a fun evening. And the night hadn't even begun.

When I tapped him on the shoulder he turned around, annoyed at the interruption, his chunky jowls ready to chop into me with a wise remark, then all at once he went white.

Everybody was looking when I said, "On the wall, fatty. Hands out, feet back and apart and make a move I don't like and you'll catch one." I let them see the rod in the Weber rig and whatever my face said, they knew I wasn't kidding. To insure the deal I nodded to Loefert, Fater and Lutz to join him and without a word they took the position. Hell, I knew they'd all be clean, but when you roust you roust and you don't give a damn. Tomorrow all hell would break loose at HQ when Reese put the squeal in, but right then I was enjoying myself. The customers had a treat, the hired help had a laugh and Al Reese damn near had a stroke when I finally got them patted down, identified and let them go back to their seats. For the others it was an old routine, but for Reese, it was strictly a new experience.

To add to it, I shoved him in the corner and made it quick. I made it loud enough so the bartender would hear it and let it go out on that grapevine that was faster than Western Union and said, "Fat boy . . . there's a girl named Paula Lees that you lay off." I looked over at Loefert and knew he was listening to every word. "If you . . . or anybody . . . bothers her I'll take your ears off. Now I'm not speaking figuratively. *I mean take your ears off.* One day see Fuchie. Remember him? Remember that goatee he had? Know what his chin looks like now? I did that, fat boy, and the same I'll do to your ears. Yell all you want and it'll be like old times in the Tombs with the rubber hose and the hard cell. Think we can't do it that way now and you aren't thinking straight."

I gave Al Reese one hard shot in the kidneys with my fist to punctuate the argument and all the breath went out of him in a long sigh and Loefert turned eyes of pure hate my way while the others played it cool and just looked away.

But they got the message.

Paula Lees got her freedom.

It was that easy. So far.

I was a cop coming home to his old turf who didn't like what he saw and decided to clean it up. I could hit the punks and take care of the unfortunate. Word would go out and maybe talking to them would be easier. Maybe.

At six I knocked at Marty's door and heard her run across the room to answer it. She had changed into a skirt and blouse, let her hair down, and the welcome home smile she gave me sent that feeling back into my stomach again. I could smell the coffee and hear chops sizzling in the kitchen and went in licking my lips.

"Hungry, Joe?" She saw my expression and added, "Don't answer that," with an even bigger smile. "Grab a beer out of the fridge. Everything'll be ready in a minute."

Damn, my place was never like this.

We ate with a peculiar intimacy neither of us wanted to mention, but it hung in the air like a wild perfume. We talked about little things, both of us prolonging the moments we had until it came to an end over coffee. Marty poured a second cup and said, "The boys will kick you out of the club if they know you've been consorting with girls."

"No more. Most of them are dead."

"Strange, isn't it?" She put the pot back on the stove and sat down. "Time goes so fast. I can remember chasing you and Larry, trying to get into the game . . . you sending me on stupid errands so I'd get lost or Larry making like he was going to scalp me with that tomahawk . . ."

"I was thinking of him before," I said.

"You miss him, don't you?"

"We were pretty close. We were those kind of brothers." I shrugged. "Life, kid."

"I know."

It had to end sooner or later so I said, "Finish your check today?"

She regretted the sudden switch as much as I did and nodded ruefully, her attitude suddenly professional. "Verbal?"

"That'll do."

"Murphy had the most to contribute," she told me. "He has some people inside their ranks and the word is that there is something hot brewing. The top men are pretty disturbed about something and have been doing a lot of traveling between New York and Chicago. Looked like a high-level series of meetings. There is a definite connection with the mob here

56

and upstate . . . they're looking out for Gus Wilder, all right, but that factor isn't of prime importance. It's something else . . . and *that* nobody is talking about."

"Still leaves us guessing," I said.

"Not quite. Orders that came from one of those meetings directed Loefert, Fater and Steve Lutz into this area. We concentrate on them, and we might find out something."

"Those guys don't break very easily," I reminded her.

"Somewhere, they always have a chink in the armor, don't they?"

"Always," I grinned. She was beginning to think like a beat cop now and not a social worker.

"Then how do we start?"

"With the first kills. It's a homicide case, baby."

"Until now nobody's talked. Nobody saw anything."

"I'm glad you're so damn confident."

"Kitten, I've been at this job a long time," I said. "There are times when they get ready. All you have to do is prod them a little."

"Okay then, ugly, I'm ready whenever you are," she laughed.

CHAPTER SEVEN

THE supper crowd had left Tony's Pizza when we got there. One couple was at the small bar, and two tables were occupied. Fat Mary was busy forcing another helping on one pair and Tony was behind the bar listening to a small transistor radio. Marty and I climbed on the stools and Tony saw us and came over grinning, the first time I saw him smile in a long time. He said hello in his rich Neapolitan accent and drew two beers automatically.

"You do nice thing for those girls, Joe," he told me. "I see them, they very glad. Terrible a woman should be on the streets and pushed around. Terrible."

"They should have kept their mouths shut or people will think the cops are getting soft."

"Ah, no. It is not like you think." He gave us a knowing glance then. "Now you two, you belong here. Good maybe that you come back, Joe. Things are bad here, very bad."

"Those killings?"

Tony nodded vigorously. "Very bad, that."

"It's another department and I'm off duty. The hell with it."

His face pulled itself into a seamy, concerned frown. "Who cares about here, Joe? The cops? They don't care. Somebody dies, so what?" He leaned forward confidentially. "That killer, he's still here. He can kill anybody."

"What can I do, Tony? Hell, I knew all the guys who got knocked off. I went to school with 'em."

Tony gave me a typical shrug. "So they're no good, well okay. But still good people here, you can bet. You oughta know. Plenty good people. They're scared, that's what."

"You scared?"

"Sure. I was scared of that stupid René Mills. I'm scared of everybody like them."

I kept my voice down. "What was with him, Tony? He was flashing money around and it was more than he ever had before. René never had the brains to set up a heist and nobody was going to just give it to him. He was a low-type punk."

Tony let his eyes rove around the place before he answered. "You know what I think? He had something on somebody. He was expectin' plenty money soon. He had it all set."

"Yeah?"

"Better'n that even. I tell you somethin', Joe. That René, he stays up all night watching that damn TV or playing cards. Always like that. Never his light go off like he's scared of the dark. Then alla sudden he got them lights out right after it gets dark. He comes down and goes up, but never a light goes on and when it does the shade is down like never before. He got somebody up there with him."

"Hiding him out?"

I got another big shrug that lasted three seconds. "Who knows?"

"Doesn't sound reasonable, Tony. Who the hell would trust René Mills?"

Tony gave me a face full of fat lip. "Suppose there's nobody else he can go to?"

"It wouldn't be René Mills, buddy."

"For whoever it was, he kicked Noisy Stuccio out, didn't he? René, he wouldn't give a pork chop to his own mother if she didn't pay. So Noisy paid him, then gets the boot. Noisy was pretty damn mad. Plenty years he live with René and pays most the bills 'cause he's scared of René. Then the boot. How about that?"

"How about that?" I repeated. "René still feeling pretty high when he got killed?"

"Sure. He thought he was all set. You gotta get that one, Joe."

"There's nothing to get."

"No?" He gave me a curious look. "Then ask that Al Reese. That fat bum, he knows. He shoves everybody. He always looking for his bite, that bum. He hooked into René, because I seen René pay him off," he confided.

I finished my beer and nudged Marta to do the same. "Okay, Tony, maybe. Just maybe, remember? I'm out of my district and I don't want to make trouble around here."

"Screw you, Joe. When you and Larry was kids, you made plenty trouble for everybody. That . . . that . . . what you call him?"

"Chief Crazy Horse," I said.

"Yeah him. Nutty Indian. Always wearing them feathers and you want to be a cop. Nobody wanted to play with you, did they?"

"I always caught the crooks," I said. I tapped the side of my head. "You had to be smart, even when you were playing."

"Now somebody ain't playing, Joe. They're going for real."

"Well, I'll see what I can do. Keep it quiet though." I pushed some change across to him and we finished our beer and left while Fat Mary was still heaping the plates of the customers that were left.

Getting into René's old apartment was no trouble. The padlock the landlord had put on opened with a sharp rap from my gun butt and the door swung open. Marta found the light switch and pulled it after making sure the shades were drawn.

The police had checked the rooms, found nothing, the landlord had made a partial attempt at cleaning it up, emptying the garbage and piling dishes in the sink, so anything of significance would have been destroyed. Like the other apartments, this was typical of a slum section. It was the front half of a partially renovated brownstone building, the flat containing a living room with a battered TV, a pair of worn mohair chairs and a couple of end tables. The bedroom was furnished with a single bed, chair and table. René's clothes came from a low cost outlet store, all bore the marks of hard usage except for two pairs of expensive shoes that hadn't been worn at all. The kitchen was a hodgepodge of rickety pieces, the dishes chipped and cracked, the closet over the refrigerator empty. But there had been plenty of groceries in there. The marks showed in the dust where cans had been stacked and a cash register slip caught in a crack was for for-

59

ty-two dollars. The landlord wasn't going to leave all that stuff for the next tenant.

When Marty came back from looking around I asked, "Find anything?"

"Possibly. Come back in the living room a minute." She pointed to the floor and indicated a series of scratches that led from one chair to the other. "We know what we're looking for . . . so do those mean anything?"

I got her point. "Somebody dragged that chair up to the other to make a bed?"

"That's right. So René *did* have somebody here." She looked at me carefully and sat on the arm of the chair. "You see the same picture, don't you?"

"Uh-huh."

"Tell it to me."

I nodded and started pacing the room. "Nobody who knew better would trust René. It had to be someone who knew him well enough to be able to handle him. René was a sharpie. So let's say this guy needs a hideout and is prepared to pay. He approaches René who kicks Noisy Stuccio out and takes this guy in. Now René starts sharpshooting. He's going to try to take this guy for his bundle and sets something up, only he makes a mistake in underestimating his new boarder. The guy gets wise and kills him.

"That gets us to Noisy Stuccio. People don't change and Noisy was a mean little punk who never liked to be second rated. He was always in somebody's business and he would have wanted to know what was going on and somehow he found out who the boarder was. If this guy knew René, then he certainly would have known Noisy. When René was killed Noisy got the score and made his bid for the loot this guy was packing."

Marta said, "And wound up the same way."

"This guy is a pure psychopath. He'll kill at the drop of a hat. He's an old experienced hand with the crazy intuitive values psychos have and can kill without leaving a trace. That's the most difficult part," I said. "There doesn't even have to be a motive. He doesn't go into wild flight that attracts attention and anybody in his way is simply disposed of."

She frowned and nibbled at a fingernail. "But Hymie Shapiro . . ."

I cut her off with, "I'll have to go back to when we were kids. Hymie and Noisy were a couple of sharpies who stuck together. Hymie used to plan little chintzy jobs and leave them up to Noisy to pull off. Could be that Noisy didn't want to move in on this by himself because he knew he wasn't capable of pulling it off alone. He always was a lippy guy with Hymie. Suppose he talked it over with Hymie and they laid it out together. Our guy would have moved out after he killed René, but they found out where he was holed up and Noisy went to see him. So the guy makes a date to pay off and instead lets Noisy have a bullet, but not before Noisy tried to insure himself staying alive by reminding the guy someone else knew the play."

"It sounds good, Joe."

"What it means is that Noisy didn't have to tell him *who* it was that knew. Our guy automatically understood, popped Noisy, then went looking for Hymie and found him."

"And that brings us up to Doug Kitchen," Marta said.

"Paula Lees saw that action. Doug saw the guy and recognized him. That's what got him killed. He started across the street to say hello, then saw what was going to happen and started to run. He was the only one shot in the back."

"Gus Wilder?"

"They all knew him. Hell, everybody around here knows everybody else, especially when they're hardcases."

I stopped pacing then and stared at the dark green surface of the dirty window shade. Marta asked, "What are you thinking of, Joe?"

"There's a hook in this someplace. I have the feeling that somebody I've talked to has fed it to me already and I can't remember what it is."

"It'll come."

"But I want it now."

"Relax," she said softly.

I turned around and grinned at her. "Sure, little Giggie. Come on and let's try it from another angle."

* * *

When we reached the street there was a slight jolt in the air, concussion from thunder far off, and the sky over Jersey turned a momentary pink. It was cooler now, the smell of rain coming in with the west breeze.

We turned south, reached the corner and saw Hal McNeil, the beat cop, just closing the door of the call box. He touched his cap in a salute and said, "Evening, Lieutenant. I was just going to look you up."

"What's doing?"

"Sergeant Brissom wants you to call him back."

"Thanks, Hal. You got anything on Loefert and his buddies?"

The cop nodded. "They're doing a lot of poking around.

61

The way it looks, they've sectioned the neighborhood off and are scouting the areas. The only one I could reach said they were looking for a strange face. A lot of drifters come through, but they weren't interested. It's somebody that would be known but hasn't been seen for a while."

"No names?"

"You know these people, sir. They aren't going to stick their necks out. Too many killings have scared them silly."

I left him talking to Marta and opened the call box and got the duty officer to put me through to Mack Brissom. "Scanlon, Mack. What's the pitch?"

"Hi, Joe. We have an opening on the action down there. Now get this bit . . . one of the Chicago hoods was picked up on an old murder second charge and the D.A. got some talk out of him because the guy hoped to drop the charge down to manslaughter."

"What's it about?" I asked him.

"The wheels inside the mob gave the go ahead signal to a group to set up one hell of a big heist and was going to take care of the cover and protection for a fifty percent bite if it came off. Well, it came off, all right, only the one guy who was holding the loot had it hijacked out of his hands by an outsider and broke up the whole deal."

"Which heist, Mack?"

"Could be the Montreal job. How this outsider got into it is anybody's guess. He could have known one of the boys, had a few drinks with him and the story came out. They'll talk to their own kind sometimes. This time, knowing they had the mob's protection, they'd figure nobody would have the guts to try to move in."

"What's the connection?"

"This guy who pulled the hijack was waiting when the driver holding the loot came out of his motel, stuck a gun in his ribs, made him drive to a spot where he had a car parked, belted him cold, took the money and ducked out."

"Recognized?"

"No, he was masked, but when he pulled the gun out a five-dollar bill and a piece of paper came out of his pocket with it. There was a phone number on the paper listed to a candy store run by Sigmund Jones in your neighborhood."

"I know the one. René Mills kept a pair of whores upstairs over it."

"Making sense?" Mack asked me.

"It's there, all right. Does Gus Wilder tie into it at all?"

"When you check the dates it does. Wilder jumped his bond two weeks before the Montreal robbery. He might have known what was cooking inside the mob and was on the spot when it happened to pick up some hideout money. Wilder was damn hot. He knew the mob wasn't going to let him stay alive if there was any indication that he'd talk about their activities. At the same time he didn't want to take a big fall. If he didn't talk, the upstate department was going after him on other charges, so the only choice he had was to jump bail."

"So the mob detailed their boys to look him up," I stated.

"That's the picture we're getting here. All he got is his brother to turn to."

I said, "He called Henry asking for five hundred bucks."

"Could be reasonable, Joe. He wouldn't want to throw hot money around just yet. That, or he asked for the money before the hijack. Check out the dates on your end, will you?"

"Tonight. I'll call you back after I see Henry Wilder."

"Right. See you later."

I hung up, closed the call box and went back to McNeil and Marta. The wind had come up a little stronger and I felt the touch of a raindrop against my face. McNeil said, "Anything I can do, sir?"

"Just keep your eyes open. I got that funny feeling that something's going to break."

"Sure will." He started to walk away, stopped and turned back. "Incidentally, Benny Loefert and Will Fater had a long talk with Al Reese tonight."

"Where?"

"In the back room at Bunny's place."

"Who passed on the word?"

"A little guy named Harry Wope."

"I know him."

"He thought you might like to know."

"Tell him thanks."

McNeil saluted again and went back to his beat.

* * *

Henry Wilder didn't appreciate the interruption. Since I saw him last he seemed to have curled up inside himself and reluctance was in every word he spoke. Gus hadn't contacted him again and as far as he was concerned he hoped he never heard from him. When I got around to asking when he had the last call he thought about it a minute, then placed the day. I ran it through my mind and let it fit the pattern. Gus' call had come after he jumped his bond and before the Montreal job, so Mack Brissom could have hit it right. Gus had no place to go and headed back to the only place he knew where he thought he'd have a reasonable place of security, buried in the anonymity of a decrepit section of the city.

So what happened? I thought. If Gus had lived here he'd know his way around and the people who lived here. It was

63

doubtful that he'd trust anybody, even his stepbrother, so be-
fore he moved in on him he'd hole up somewhere else long
enough to feel Henry out. Trouble was then, René Mills saw
him and knew about him skipping his bond and made a deal
with him. If Gus was packing the Montreal money, René
would have wanted it for himself and set up the scene to grab
it. He would have had Gus move in with him where he could
be on top of everything and his greed bought his own death.

It fitted, all right, even to Doug Kitchen. Doug was a gre-
garious kind of guy who knew everybody and was always
there with a ready hello and handshake. Gus was gone from
the neighborhood long enough to warrant a greeting upon his
return, and Doug died because he recognized him. From little
acorns do big oaks grow. A corny cliché, but true.

We told Henry Wilder good night and went downstairs to
the street again. The sidewalks were just starting to take on a
sheen from the light rain that had started to fall. While we
walked I gave it to Marta in detail and let her process it mentally the way I did and her conclusion agreed with mine.

"I think you have it, Joe."

I shook my head and turned my collar up against the
wind. "I don't know," I said. "Something's loose in the picture. I want everything to fit tight."

"Does it always?"

I grinned and looked at her. "Most of the time."

We got to Papa Jones' candy store as he was closing. Most
of the lights were out and he was stuffing his daily receipts
into his pocket when we walked in. He gave Marta a smile,
but when he saw me his face went suddenly tight and his
shoulders jumped under his too-loose suitcoat. He was remembering me from a long time ago and the time when he
broke my nose with the awning rod and I promised to come
back and tear him up but never got farther than breaking his
front window with a rock.

"Ease off, Papa." I said. "The past is past. It's different
now." To prove it I let him see my badge in the wallet and
his face went sideways in a curious change of expression. He
finally swallowed hard and croaked, "Joe?"

"Nobody else."

"A . . . cop?"

"Haven't you heard? I've been around a few days."

"I . . . been out," he said. "Ronnie's been taking care . . .
of things."

Marta turned around and explained, "Ronnie's his nephew."

Papa Jones glanced at both of us nervously, his fingers
fumbling with the buttons of his coat. Cops always make
them nervous. "So . . . what do you want with me? I'm closing up."

"Remember Gus Wilder, Papa?"

His false teeth clicked and he nodded. "Sure, I remember him."

"See him lately?"

"He left here a long time ago. He . . ."

"I didn't ask that."

Papa Jones took on new confidence then. "I ain't seen him since."

"Know him pretty well, Papa?"

He tried to get my angle, but couldn't figure it and said, "So enough. He used the phone here all the time. Bought cigarettes and things like that."

"Phone number been changed lately?"

He scowled and shook his head. "Same since you kids used it. The phone got changed, but not the number, why?"

"No reason."

"So what's the phone? Everybody uses it. That René Mills, Stuccio . . . hell, the whole neighborhood uses it. Who got their own phones around here?" he demanded defensively.

"Sure, Papa. Well look, if you see this Wilder, you call us, hear?"

"Yeah," he said, but didn't mean it. "Why don't you ask his brother where he is?"

"That'll be taken care of. Just do like I said or I'll keep that old promise. You remember it?"

He did, all right. "Damn bunch of bums, you kids were," he muttered. Then his face got a little pale and he watched me closely.

I grinned and took Marta's hand. "Come on, kid."

Papa Jones slammed and locked the door the minute we were out and yanked the shade down fast. Marta said, "You make quite an impression."

"I always did with him."

"What did you make out of it, Joe?"

"It's tightening up. Like he said, everybody uses the phone. Gus Wilder could have done just that and been spotted by René. He would have waited until Gus came out so Papa Jones wouldn't see them together and tapped him then. It even explains why Gus had the phone number in his pocket . . . a secondary number he knew in the neighborhood if he wanted to make a contact in case his brother's phone was tapped."

The sky rumbled again and the lightning flashes moved closer. The main force of the rain was starting to sweep in on the city, driving the inhabitants indoors to their sanctuaries. We hugged the sides of the buildings to get out of the bite of the storm, heading across to Bunny's place. The street was empty, traffic light, just an occasional cab going by, a couple of trucks, a few private cars looking for a way out of the place.

I heard the curious slap of lead against the bricks before I realized what it was. The sound behind it was muffled in the wind, but it could have come from only one direction. I grabbed Marta's arm, yanked her into a run and dashed across the street and just as we reached the middle I felt her spin a little bit and let out a yell and knew she was hit. I cursed softly, got to the sidewalk and flattened up against the building there with my gun out and ready.

"Joe . . ."

"Where'd it get you?"

She reached up and touched the top of her shoulder. The cloth was torn and a faint tinge of red darkened the edges of it. "It . . . isn't much."

"Stay down out of sight. He's in one of these buildings. I'm going in and if I flush him out, hold a gun on him. Think you can make it?"

"Don't worry." She grabbed my hand. "Should you . . . go in alone?"

"There isn't time to raise anybody else. I know these damn buildings and every way in and out of them. You do what I told you to."

Before she could answer me I ran up into the brownstone beside me, taking the steps in two leaps, shoved the door open and went up the stairs. There wasn't an empty apartment on the block and nobody was letting a killer use his place for a firing range. Those shots came from a rooftop and somewhere the guy behind the gun was looking for an escape hatch.

I made the roof at the top of the four stories and came out into the rain from a rusted metal fire door built into the kiosk, the squeak of the hinges like a shrill scream in the darkness. I hit the pebbled surface of the roof and rolled behind the protection of a weather-eroded brick chimney, my eyes probing the black for any movement, any outline of a person.

Too many times I had played these same games on these same rooftops. I was no stranger to these parts at all and it was like old times when the bunch of us turned rooftops into rolling countrysides doing the cowboy and Indian routine or played out the cops and robbers game. I could almost feel Larry beside me, old Chief Crazy Horse, or hear René's sharp whisper from near the cornice, and Hymie Shapiro's nervous cough giving away our position to the ones taking the opposite role. Our guns had been cap pistols then, or rubber band gimmicks . . . but now they were real and the game a lethal one.

I heard him before I saw him. I heard the wrench of metal and the curse and grinned because I knew what had happened. Fire escapes twenty years out of date didn't hold any more and the bolts were loose in the cement joints of the brick edging. It all looked good from below and provided a quick getaway . . . until you tried it and found out lousy contractors had never set them right, the weather had eaten them loose and too many kids wrenching at them had finished the job. Anybody trying to climb down them needed a lot of nerve.

The lightning blossomed again and I saw his outline skirting the back edge of the building at a crouching run and I fired a shot into the air. He looked back, showing the white oval of his face, triggered a shot in my direction, then he grabbed the two loops of the iron rails that hooked into the building and slithered over the top.

I ran then. I took a chance he was alone and crossed between the chimneys and the TV antennas, ducking under the clotheslines strung around the place and reached the spot where he disappeared.

Below me the night was too shadowed, the intensity of the black too deep to pick out any movement and I had to take my chances. I felt the rails under my hands, swung a leg over and felt for the rungs when I heard the scream, a startled yell that twisted into a cry of pure terror and was cut off abruptly as a body hit the concrete yard below with a sickening thud.

There was no sense trying it then. I went back the way I came, past the curious faces looking out the doors at me, ducking back when I let them see the badge in my hand to cut off their questions. I found him lying face up, dead as hell, splashed in red over the garbage and ground, the gun still in his pocket and the fright-look plain on his face. Will Fater wasn't going anyplace any more.

But I was. I wanted to see what that talk was about he had with Al Reese and Benny Loefert in the back of Bunny's place.

CHAPTER EIGHT

WHEN the lab crew finished and the body was carted away I took Marta back to her apartment. The doctor had dressed the minor flesh wound, a sear across her shoulder that bothered her more because it ripped her clothes than damaged her.

She showered, changed into a housedress and made us some coffee, still a little shook up from the initial experience of getting shot at.

The bell rang and Marta went to the door. Captain Oliver and Inspector Bryan walked in, faces impassive. Marta poured them some coffee and they sat down, glad to be in out of the rain. Captain Oliver said, "This is bad, Joe. The pressure's coming in from upstairs again."

"So we scrubbed one hood. Why the beef?"

"Voters' complaints. This is a tight little political group. Practically everybody is registered at the polls and can be swung one way or another."

"This is police work, not a political football," I said.

"Maybe so, but when the papers get this it'll be murder. They're all hot over this upstate deal and to have it in their back yard can make us look silly. You got any idea where you're going?"

I nodded. "In a way."

"It better be more than that," Bryan growled. "We're ready to pull a house-to-house search for Gus Wilder next."

"Try it and you'll have every damn door slammed in your face," I reminded him. "You'll need a warrant to get into every apartment and by that time our boy will be gone. You think this whole neighborhood doesn't feel what's going on? It doesn't take much to put two and two together. They know I'm here and nosing around. They know who I've been talking to and what's been said. They can read the papers and draw a picture."

"We're not revealing Fater's identity yet."

"Just the same, they know it was me on that roof. From now on, I'm not just a cop on a date with a local girl. They'll know I'm here on an assignment and will clam up tight. I want a couple of more days to do it my way. There's something lousy about this whole thing. It doesn't stick. It has a hitch in it."

"Like what, Joe?"

"I don't know."

"Two days then," Inspector Bryan reminded me.

"That'll do it," I said.

When they left I finished my coffee and sat looking out over the street that had been my playground. I had my feet up on the windowsill watching the rain beat against the glass and Marta came over and perched on the arm of the chair, her hand absently stroking the back of my neck.

"Thinking, Joe?"

I reached out and put my arm around her. Beneath the sheer cloth of the dress she was a warm, vibrant thing full of

68

life. My fingers kneaded the flesh of her hip and I felt her react to my touch, involuntarily drawing closer. The dead lay outside, but inside myself that knot started again in my stomach and ran up through my shoulders into an explosion I couldn't stop.

"Should I tell you what I'm thinking of?"

"I think I know," she said.

She came down into my arms slowly, her mouth lovely and moist, meeting mine in a gentle touch that said hello after a long, long time and fought with the years in between and wiped them away in a violent burst of passion. Her tongue was a separate entity that spoke a new language I had never heard and always missed without realizing it.

My hands had held a shield and gun too long to be gentle. They were rough when they pushed away fabric to feel the silky smoothness of bare skin beneath, and she never uttered a sound except to moan softly and give herself fully to my inquisitiveness.

There was no policewoman here now . . . no little Giggie with childish notions; she was a woman enmeshed in emotions suppressed too long and we were both finding the answers with the complete naïveté of kids endowed with the prowess of adults. It was a ritual of honesty and total love that happened and was consummated despite the tension of murder and a storm that attempted to match our own violence, a ritual of absolute abandonment to something we seemed to know would always occur. We handled each other with a frenzy of desire, searching, finding, enjoying until all that was left was utter exhaustion.

Outside the storm lashed the city, but it was an hour before we heard it. Marty stirred beside me, came awake quickly when she knew I was too. "Joe . . ."

"I have to leave, kid."

"Why?"

"He's still loose."

"Who is he, Joe?"

"I don't know yet. I can't be sure."

"Can you tell me?"

"No."

"Then I want to go with you."

"Orders, sugar. You stay. Your part is done. I can't use you in the job now."

"Please, Joe."

"No choice, Marty. It's guns now. I don't want you in the middle. It's all changed, and I want you where I know I can come back to you."

"Will you?"

69

I turned and kissed her, felt her tremble slightly and said, "I'll be back. I have to. We started too long ago to let it end now. It's you and me now, Marty. We're back where we started, but it's better and we have a lot to look forward to. We're on the straight side and can be the builders. I want you, Marty."

Very simply, she said, "You have me, Joe. It's always been that way. There never has been anyone else."

"I know it," I grinned.

*   *   *

A kill stirs things up. It's like having a winning ball club. The fans gather to talk about it, to speculate and chew it to pieces. Donavan's place was packed and so was Bunny's, but the one I was looking for wasn't in either one. But that wasn't the end. There were a lot of places he could go to.

And I looked in them all. I put the word out and let them take it as they liked. I was a cop with a name he wanted and everybody knew it. It wasn't going to take long. There was always somebody who wanted a favor or some heat taken off and they'd show sooner or later. While I waited I kept on looking and knew the others were all watching, knowing I was there and it wasn't over yet, not by a long sight.

It was little Harry Wope who found me. He was buried in the shadows of the corner drug store and whistled as I walked past, stepping far enough out into the light so I'd recognize him and when I moved beside him, sought out the shadows again.

"Scanlon . . ."

"Hello, Harry."

"It was Will Fater who got it, wasn't it?"

"Everybody else is guessing."

"Not me. I knew what they were gonna pull off. I told you."

"What else do you know?"

"How much money did Fater have on him?"

"A couple hundred bucks. That's all."

"He should have had more," Harry said. "Al Reese promised him more. I heard him. That stupid Fater, for five grand he'd shoot himself. He had a big reputation, that one did. He never said nothin', but he had it."

"We know, Harry."

"So Reese said five grand."

"Where would he get it?" I asked him.

"He said he was coming into it. Soon, too. He had Will all worked up. He would'na taken the job on if he wasn't sure."

"And where is Reese now?"

"That's what I wanted to tell you. I seen him by Grafton's place. Over two blocks and . . ."

"I know where it is," I said.

"Reese, he got out of a car and was walking," Harry Wope told me. "He had on a raincoat and was carrying an umbrella, but I seen his face when he was getting out. A couple of people came along and he ducked down behind that umbrella like he didn't want to be seen, but I knew who he was."

"See where he went?"

"Raining too hard. He was up near Paula Lees' place when I couldn't see him no more. I didn't wait around, anyway. I went looking for you."

"Okay, Harry, thanks. You get the hell out of here and don't mention seeing me."

"Sure enough. Not a word. You give that Al Reese what he needs, huh?"

"Don't worry."

I waited until Harry was out of sight before crossing the street. I knew where Grafton's place was. Twenty-five years ago I had run errands for the guy, delivered his orders and fought for my right to sell papers on the corner he occupied.

Fifty feet from the intersection a late-model Chevvy sedan was parked, the doors locked. After an initial glance at it I walked on down the street, casing every building as I went. Any darkened doorway or unlighted window could hide a killer behind it. One try was made, another was possible. Will Fater's try for me was a money deal, not the original one.

But there was a tie-in there too. If Gus Wilder came into the section, Al Reese could have known about it. Political bosses had to keep their fingers on the pulse of every movement in their area. If there was a bite to be taken out of a money pie Al Reese would want his and anybody standing in his way had to be taken out.

The possibility was plain now. René Mills lost his shot at the dough. . . . Reese wasn't going to miss his. He could have promised René protection for a price, and even if René got killed for his trouble Reese was going to push it. He wouldn't put himself in the same class as René, not Al Reese. He had power and cover from the party whom he represented. Anybody circulating in his bailiwick was going to pay off no matter who they were.

Up ahead was Paula Lees' apartment.

Cute deal, Al, *I thought.* A guy is holed up and wanting a woman. You make the arrangements for him and catch him

71

with his pants down and put the screws to him. Maybe you'd be doing it right now and I could nail you both at once.

I took the gun out, checked the load in the cylinders and cut in when I came to the worn sandstone stoop. I would have gone up the steps if the sudden brilliance of the lightning flash hadn't turned night into day and outlined a quick movement from behind the railing that guarded the basement entrance to the tenement across the street.

This time I moved as fast as they did, not quickly, just deliberately. As far as they were concerned, I was just another pedestrian. I had stayed out of the glow of the street lights from force of habit and my pause by Paula's apartment could have been accidental if they hadn't seen me with the gun in my hand. I bent down, made like I was flipping water from my cuffs, pulled the collar of my trench coat tighter around my neck and ambled on like a guy walking aimlessly after fighting with his wife.

I didn't look back to see if the act worked. I kept on going until I reached the corner, found the alley in between the stores and squeezed between the garbage cans and refuse cartons stacked shoulder high until I reached the fence, then climbed over it.

For a second I had the funny feeling that it was the game again. A long time ago the bunch of us had come through this same alley over the same fence to scramble through the basement of the apartment to get away from Ralph Callahan who was after us for some piece of hell we had just raised. Now it was the other way around and I was the cop.

The cellar doors set at a forty-five degree angle were still the same, boards warped, braces loose and two hinges rusted away. I pulled one up, went down the steps with the light of my pencil flash showing the way, seeing the same old asbestos-wrapped furnace sitting in the middle of the room like a dead, dirty idol, the coal bin on the left gaping blackly. It was neater now than the last time, probably because a fire inspector had checked the premises and squeezed the landlord.

A flight of rickety steps led to the first floor. The door was locked, but a steady push with my shoulder snapped the lock and sent the door slamming open against the wall with a noise that would have gotten anyone alerted.

But it didn't. It was drowned in the resonating blast of gunfire from the floor above that rolled through the building with punctuated hammering that was sharper than the echoes they made. They came too fast to identify the caliber, but at least three were going, then two, one, and all that was left was the sharp smell of cordite and a dull reverberation that bounced from the walls until it died out in the yells of the neighbors and the sound of a woman screaming for the police somewhere outside.

I stayed close to the wall, took the stairs two at a time, nearly fell over a body and in stumbling saved my neck. A shot from above snapped down, missing me by an inch, powdering plaster and wood chips into my face. Above me, feet went up the staircases, paused, went up again and stopped.

There were too many times when a cop had things taken out of his hands. I had to get him. I took each landing with the .38 ready to reach out for a target, went up the stairs waiting to catch one myself and damn near eager for the opportunity to swap one for the other, but none came my way. The door to the roof was open and without thinking about it I went through into the rain and dove for the shelter of the parapet.

No bullet sought me out. No feet ran from me. There was just that deathly stillness and the sensation that I was all alone. I got up and walked along the edge, peering down into the alleyway. A garbage can rattled, then a board·creaked from the fence and the silhouette of a man showed briefly as he slithered over it. I got off a quick shot, even though I knew the range was too long and the light too bad, then went back down the stairs.

Steve Lutz was dead on the steps near the landing, half his head splattered over the wall. Beamish lay face down near the door of Paula Lees' apartment, his blood puddled all over the floor from a hole in his throat. I kicked the door open not knowing what I was going to find. The light was on in the kitchen and directly under it, half sprawled in a chair, was the fat lump of what was left of Al Reese. The bullet that had torn into his chest had left a fist-sized hole in his back and if the signs were right it had been deliberately placed by somebody who had stood in the doorway leading to the bedroom.

She lay on the bed, eyes wide and staring, her body twisted in the agony of torture applied by an expert in the art of taking pleasure from someone else's pain. She should have been dead. I thought she was. Apparently the other person thought she was too. The motion of her chest was barely perceptible, a minor spasmodic movement that was involuntary on her part, an effort of a human body hanging on to life.

When her lips moved I bent over and said, "Paula . . . it's Joe Scanlon."

She moved her mouth in an effort to repeat my name.

"Paula . . . who was it?"

Her voice was a weak whisper I could hardly hear. I bent my head closer and heard her say, "Al . . . was going to

73

. . . let me . . . work. He . . . he said so. He wanted a . . . favor."

"What favor, Paula?"

"Meet . . . somebody here," she finally got out.

"Who, Paula, who?"

Instead of answering she said, "Al . . . was supposed to . . . come first. But . . . *he* did." Her breathing came in a series of short gasps and she had trouble speaking. *"He* was . . . terrible. *He* did . . ." Whatever she was remembering stopped the flow of words.

After a few seconds her mouth moved again. "Al . . . came in. He . . . sat down. I tried to scream . . . then . . . then *he* hit me with something."

Quietly, I asked again, "Who, Paula?"

Her eyes came back from the limbo they had been looking into. The glassy look vanished momentarily and they moved to focus on mine. I reached out to touch her and she drew back, the blood suddenly spurting from the ugly gash in her temple and her mouth opened to scream. The sound never came out. She died with her face contorted, mouth twisted in terror and in her eyes a hopeless look of staring into death itself.

The first squad car pulled to the curb outside and I heard heavy feet on the stairs. They came in and photographed the scene, took my statement, carted out the bodies past the group on the sidewalk who braved the rain to satisfy their morbidity, then Oliver and Bryan took me aside and it was like the first night when I was called in to look at the remains of Doug Kitchen lying on the sidewalk.

Captain Oliver said, "We can't let this one ride, Joe. It's wide open now. We're going to have our heads handed to us and yours comes in on a silver platter."

"Screw it."

"You were there," Inspector Bryan told me bleakly.

"Sure, too late. I had no choice. I told you I saw somebody across the street. Let's say it was Beamish and Loefert. Al Reese set up a date with our killer and had them along for insurance. Only trouble was, the killer was wise, popped Reese and waited for Beamish and Loefert and got them too."

Bryan nodded. "We'll have to wait for ballistics to run a test, but the bullets in Beamish and Loefert are the same calibre as the one that went into the wall over your head. We haven't found the one that went through Reese yet. None of them came from those hoods' guns."

We stood there in the rain with nothing much to say until Captain Oliver coughed and without looking at me, said,

"You'll have to come off it, Joe. We can't take the heat that's going to come."

"You gave me two days, remember?"

"We'll have to take it back. If the Lees dame had talked maybe we could have had something, but we're still up in the air."

"Let me have tonight then."

"No more," Bryan said abruptly. "It won't do any good, but you have that much. Now let's get the hell out of this rain."

CHAPTER NINE

I HAD to walk it out. I could never go back to where I left her waiting for me until it was finished. I circled the perimeter of the place that had given me birth and raised me with the smell of it in my nose and the feel of it in my fingers and thought about what had happened and tugged at the string that led to the end, and all I could do was unravel an unending ball of confusion.

At the corner I stopped and opened the call box, rousted Mack Brissom from the coffee he was having over his late reports and gave him the details of the night. He said, "Tough, Joe."

"That's the way it goes, Mack. We checked out your inquiry about Gus Wilder and . . ."

"Forget it," he said, "Wilder's out."

"What?"

"His body turned up three hours ago. He knocked himself off with a .22 target pistol the same day he was supposed to appear for trial. I got a Coroner's report right here on my desk. He's been dead all this time."

"Damn," I said. I hung up and shut the door on the call box and went back down the street.

The knots were in the string now and it was pulled tight. It was a different string, and the knots were tied in an odd direction, but they made the shape of a noose and were a terrible thing to look at.

I knew where I was going now. It was the only place I could go. No, Paula Lees hadn't talked, but had said something without a word that was more important than anyone else. She had told me the same thing Papa Jones had told me that I didn't want to hear and deliberately let it pass.

A lot of things spoke the truth. The simple fact that I was here again was part of it. I couldn't help coming back either. I reached the corner and walked down to where the police car was parked and had the officer drive me to the street I hated to see. Since that morning, the construction crews had begun to move in their equipment that would demolish the whole place to make way for a new project building financed by the taxpayers and turned into a handsome garbage pit by the same people the housing project dispossessed.

I got out of the car slowly, dismissed the driver and stood looking up at the darkened windows of the apartment. The cold rain pelted the glass, making it look like a black mirror, an evil, nasty pair of eyes in the face of an evil, nasty building. There was something disgusting about it all, something foul and dirty, even unthinkable.

Up there, behind that darkened window, I had to kill myself. Up there I'd know what it would be like to lie dead, knowing the feeling and sight of featureless expression, the laxity of death.

The gun in my pocket seemed too heavy, so I just took it out and crossed the street with it in my hand. The front door was open. So was the inside one. Behind it was the yawning, cavernous mouth of the pitch black stairway and corridor.

One flight up and to the front.

In my mind I was picturing my face on the floor, half turned into the light, eyes partially open and the jaw slack. All consciousness gone. All conscience gone too. Nothing left. Just dead.

Under my feet the carpet was worn, and each step brought a musty, aged smell closer. From habit born long ago I stepped over the step that had pulled away from the wall, and as a kid would, counted my way toward the landing.

Four more to go. Then three, two, one and I was there. The door was ten feet away. I didn't hurry. I wasn't in a hurry to see what I looked like dead.

So I went slowly and when I had the knob under my hand I thumbed back the .38 Positive and thought how stupid it all was. And how it started. In a way, it had two starting points, but the first was last and the last first. At the last second I was thinking back over the simplicity and stupidity of the whole thing.

I pushed the door open with the nose of the gun. I didn't need a light. One of the kerosene lanterns from the construction site outside was enough to make a pale orange glow enough to see by. He was sprawled out in an old beat up chair, the smoke from his cigarette drifting up lazily from his mouth.

I said, "Hello, Larry."

And the one they had called Chief Crazy Horse, my own twin I had thought was dead a long time ago, turned and looked at me with that wild grin he could always muster up and said, "I was wondering when you'd turn up, Joe."

"I'm here."

"Too bad."

"Is it?"

He dragged on the butt and flipped the remains of it across the floor. "You're on the spot now, aren't you?"

"I am." It was a statement, not a question.

He looked at me and shrugged. "You should have known better."

"I wish I had." I paused and stared at him, seeing my own face reflected there. As long as he didn't move or speak, it was me. Physically, there was no difference. Oh, a little, maybe, but time had done different things to both of us. Only mentally were we different and the gap between us was vast.

Chief Crazy Horse. He had been aptly named.

It wasn't easy to face, but it was true. He was crazy. He always had been.

"Why, Larry?"

"Does it make a difference?"

"Maybe."

He grinned again and stretched. "Listen, brother of mine, you got your ways and I got mine. We're still brothers, ain't we? Like I said, you're on a spot."

"You didn't answer me, Larry."

"Joe . . . come off it. You mean why what?"

"Start at the beginning, Larry, or shall I do it for you?"

"Let's hear your version, brother. You always were the smart one. You liked to play the cop part and now you're doing it right. So tell me. I'd like to hear about it."

The gun was warmer now, nearly too warm to hold. It was a living thing there in my hand, held low at my side.

"You always enjoyed the wild life, Larry."

"True. So who wants to be a slob? You think I could take this place like them others out there? Man, I wanted more than that."

"There were other ways of getting it."

"Not for me, brother boy. After I faked getting myself knocked off by a land mine during the war, I picked up a record fast. Black market crap and all that under a real hero's name who got checked off as a deserter. I wasn't the employable type. Besides, I didn't go for that eight-to-five routine." He grinned again as if I understood. "But you ain't telling me your version, Joe."

77

"Suppose I pick it up from before Montreal."

"Go ahead."

"You tried a small bank job and bungled it. You were on the inside with the wrong people and got wind of the Montreal deal and hijacked the money from the driver who carried it."

"Right so far, kid, but it wasn't me who bungled the job. It was the idiot I had with me who got scared."

I ignored him and said, "You made your way down here, coming home to hide like a salmon going upstream to breed where he was born himself."

For a second Larry scowled, trying to understand the analogy, then broke into a chuckle and looked at me. "You got a way with words, boy."

"Why here, Larry?"

"Where else? It seemed good enough. It would have been great if I didn't make that call from Papa Jones' place. I never figured the old goat would know me, but I guess he did. Then René spotted me and there I was." He looked at the ceiling absently. "That dirty pig tried to screw me out of the cash. What got me was he thought I didn't know what he was up to. Man, I was on to him from the first. Like that wasn't bad enough, old Noisy Stuccio had to make a go at it with Hymie backing him up." Larry glanced over at me and added, "They died easy, boy. Real easy."

"Doug Kitchen didn't."

"What the hell . . . if he sounded off I'd have had it. Nobody else knew I was around."

"Al Reese did."

Larry grunted, his mouth twisting into a sneer. "That louse! Sure, René put him wise to get some cover and Reese was going to hit me up for a bundle. He got hit, all right. A permanent hit." He swung around in his chair and curled a leg under him, nothing showing in his face at all. It was still just a game to him, a rooftop game that could end when he wanted to call it quits. "Hell, Joe, he woulda got to me sooner, only he didn't know where I was. I had to get out of René's place and I came here. Maybe he figured it out the same way you did, but he ran me down. If he had the chance he would have bumped me, only then he never would have gotten the money at all. So he sits here and gases with me . . . tries to soften me up by paying my way with some hooker named Paula Lees."

"And you made the date," I stated.

"Sure, why not? I knew what he was setting me up for. You think I didn't know the mob had men in this neighborhood? Hell, brother boy, I seen 'em. I knew the word was out. I just couldn't figure how they got the answer."

"You aren't that hard to decipher, Larry."

He frowned again, his mouth tight while he thought about it. "Balls," he said.

"You knew I was here, didn't you?"

The frown went into an immediate grin, a kid having a change of pace in the conversation. "Sure I did. I seen you outside looking up here once when you were with little Giggie. Big broad now, that one."

"Know why I was here?"

His shrug was elaborate. "Sure," he repeated. "Cops and kills go together. This is your turf too, brother boy. They'd call you in for it. Didn't they?"

"That's right."

"So what's the complaint? Who got bumped? You think anybody's gonna miss them slobs?"

"That isn't the point, Larry."

"Nuts," he grunted.

"Where's the money, kid?"

His smile was slow and came on as if I had told a joke. "You want a hunk too?"

"I don't want any part of it at all."

"No? Well, it's where nobody can ever find it, brother boy."

"What do you bet?"

Whatever was in my tone reached him and he stiffened in the chair. "What're you getting at, Joe?"

"You never change, Larry. In some things you never change. Just as you came back to where it all started, your habits are the same. Want me to tell you where it is? In the same place you always used to hide things when you were a kid, in that space under the stairs we found together when we were about ten years old. You think I don't remember it, but I can take you right to it and pull those boards off and show you whatever it was you hid there. A couple of suitcases maybe?"

The knuckles of his fingers were tight around the arm of the chair, biting deep into the padding. His one secret that he guarded so well was no secret at all and he was coming apart right before my eyes.

"Damn you," he said.

"So it's over, Larry. Let's go easy, okay?"

"You . . . my brother . . . you're gonna try and . . ."

"Larry," I said, "you tried to kill me earlier. You didn't care if I was your brother or not."

His voice was cold, toneless. It sounded to me the way it must have sounded to René, Stuccio and the others. I wondered if he yelled that wild Indian yell with them like he did with Doug Kitchen that Paula Lees heard and told me about. That was the little thing that had bugged me. That yell. He used to do it when he was playing his Indian games. *I should have known then.*

He said, "You should have minded your own business."

"I was, Larry," I said softly.

He didn't look like me then. It wasn't my face for a second. It was somebody else, a person I had never known and would never know. It was the face the dead men had seen, the face that had tortured Paula Lees into submission and now it was looking at me.

"I'm going, Joe."

"With me," I said.

"Not with you. Alone. I've always been alone."

Before the words were out I knew what would happen. It was the one thing I had forgotten about. *"Chief Crazy Horse,"* I said. "You really are crazy."

His hand was a blur of motion as he dug for the gun, the professional killer going into the act he knew best. But he forgot the old axiom of not being able to outdraw a man who already has a gun in his hand.

My own training and instincts reacted with his own and I felt the .38 buck once in my fist and a small, bluish dot suddenly centered in the middle of his forehead, snapping his head back with a jerk. Very slowly my twin sighed and sat down in the chair again.

And very slowly the face of the man I didn't know turned into the face of one I knew all too well as it relaxed in the deep black of death.

Outside the rain would be a cleansing thing. There was a woman waiting for me to come back. There were people to be told that the terror was over. But it was going to take a lot of rain to wash everything away and a lot of woman to make me forget the memory of the night.

It would come, though.

I went back to where I started from, turned my back to it and walked to where the future was waiting for me.

MAN ALONE

CHAPTER ONE

I CAME out of the cellarway to the street corner and stood there while the rain bit into my face. It was cold and wind-whipped, but it was good. It had a fresh, clean smell, and the rivulets that ran down into my collar had a living feel about them.

Behind me the little guy in the substreet doorway said, "See you," and threw a friendly wave.

I winked at him. "Thanks, Mutt."

"Sure, anytime," he said, and slipped the door shut.

Across the street a cab disgorged a passenger, and when I whistled the driver fingered an okay sign, swept around in a screaming U turn, opened the door for me and took off again in a seemingly single operation.

The crowd was coming out of the Criminal Courts Building now, the photogs in front holding their cameras under their coats while they yelled and waved to the press cars at the curb to look awake. Behind them were the vultures who made the spectator's seats home, and from their outraged clacking you could sense that they were annoyed at not having something to feed on.

The cabbie looked forward to take it all in, then half turned his head to ask over his shoulder, "You been at the trial, Mac?"

I leaned back against the cushions and stared at the ceiling. "I was there," I said.

"He gonna sit in it?"

"Not this time." I cranked the window all the way down to smell the fresh air again. "Take me to Sixth and Forty-ninth."

Ahead the cabbie seemed to stretch up to meet my eyes in his rear-view mirror and when he spoke his voice was almost out of control.

"*What!*"

"Sixth and Forty-ninth," I repeated.

Unbelievingly, the driver shook his head. "No . . . I mean about the trial. What'd you say?"

"You heard me."

"Yeah, but what'd he do . . . cop a plea? Or did they knock it down to second degree?"

"Nothing like that at all, friend."

The cabbie stretched again, trying to make contact with my eyes, but it was too dark and the mirror too small. He fidgeted, then: "Well, come on, Mac, what gives? All you've been hearing this last week is that trial. Papers. Radio. TV. Everybody I pick up hashes it over. So what happens. He escape or something?"

I waited a second before I said quietly, "You might call it that."

"Brother!" There was a degree of awe in his voice.

I said, "The jury turned in a *not guilty* verdict."

This time he whistled between his teeth and said, *"Brother,"* half under his voice.

"You don't like it?"

With a typical New Yorker's contempt for what was already past news, he shrugged and shoved a cigarette in his mouth. "Hell, who cares? Me . . . I just can't see how they figger, that's all."

"No?" I waited a second, then added, "Why?"

A one-sided shrug almost explained it. "Look," he said, "the guy's a cop who's supposed to run down a big fish, only when he catches him he takes a pay-off instead. Then when he gets tagged with the loot in his pocket he's suspended from the department and while he sweats out an investigation he makes big noises about getting the fish who fingered him."

"So."

"So he makes the noises stick when he shoots up the guy he started out to get legally. He sure picked a big one to burn down."

"He did?"

"Listen, that Leo Marcus was a real front-marching big wheel. Brother, six slugs in the puss he gets and all head on. No face yet."

The cab careened around a truck, knifed to a pole position at a red light and waited impatiently. The driver reached up to readjust the mirror so he could see me a little better and sucked on his butt until the cab was blue with smoke.

"Sure can't figger it out though," he repeated. "It was open and shut all the way around."

My voice was real cold now. "It was?"

"Why, sure. They catch him on the spot, his gun, his belly full of booze, witnesses to the beef and no two-bit witnesses either. How'd he get out of it?"

"The jury said not guilty."

82

"Man, man! I bet that judge did take the hide off'n them jurors. Would I sure like to have heard that."

"He tore them up."

Up front the driver began to laugh a little. "Their angle I can see now. The jury, I mean. Sure, I can even understand 'em. And you know, I don't mind a bit. That Marcus took plenty of my loot when he was running the old cab protection racket. Yep, I can sure see their angle now." He grinned into the mirror. "You too?"

I leaned into the corner, away from the eyes. "You tell me."

"They figure he did a public service. So big that they let a fractured killer cop out for an airing. So now let him shoot the rest of 'em up."

I closed the window up against the rain, leaned forward and handed a bill across the back of the seat. "I'll get out here."

"But you wanted . . ."

"This is fine."

The cabbie's fingers felt the bill as he eased over toward the curb, batted the flag and clicked a quarter change out of the box on the dash. He stopped, then turned to pass the change over. It took a second, then something happened to his face that made it tighten around the mouth and he had trouble getting enough breath to say, "You're . . . Regan."

I nodded. "That's right. The killer cop."

"Hell, Mac . . ."

"Forget it. Keep the change."

* * *

I walked three blocks north, leaning into the sharp sting of the rain, and on 49th turned east until I reached Donninger's. It wasn't much of a place; a few food specialties and the drinks were good, but what made it tick was its place on the grapevine and the dial phone at every wall table.

It was still too early for the supper crowd, but the day bunch from the tabloids were lined up at the bar swearing at editors and policy makers over the one for the road. It was tomorrow's news that was important, not today's. Today's had been shot down and buried in ink, then folded into neat paper caskets to be handed over to the procession that would follow it avidly. Only the unborn news-child of tomorrow was important.

I walked behind them, flipping the water from my hat brim, squinting until my eyes could adjust to the cool darkness of the place. Jerry Nolan was in the far booth, crouched over a plate of spaghetti, a late paper in his hand. I looked for his partner, Al Argenio, but didn't see him.

I said, "Hi, Jerry."

He didn't even look up. "You're poison, Regan."

"Personal or departmental?"

A frown wrinkled the corners of his eyes, then he sat back and glanced up at me, the mark of his trade plain on his face. *Sgt. Nolan, detective division. The law. And nothing was really important except the law.* He pointed the paper at the chair opposite him. "Sit down, Regan."

"Thanks."

"I'm not being friendly. We just have to square some things away."

"That's going to take doing."

"Yeah." His eyes got narrow. "I don't see how, but it'll get done."

I started to grin at him. It had been a long time coming, but at least I could still find some funny things left.

"Don't clown around about it, Regan. It's no joke."

The tight, stiff feeling I had had so long seemed to ooze out of me, a painful, swollen abscess of emotion finally gently bursting, still leaving the toxin, but obtaining relief.

I said, "That's not right, Jerry. It *is* a joke. A damn big joke at that. Here the department didn't bother to press an investigation on the graft charge because the brass figured me for a gone goose. I was a dead man to them." My grin got bigger. "Now a charge will look ridiculous. They'll have to say I took money that led to my committing a murder that never happened. The papers will really go for that one."

"Maybe."

"What do you think of it, Jerry? You think the jury loused it up?"

I knew what he wanted to say but he had too much cop in him; too much respect for the "due processes" to spell it out. The paper tapped against the edge of the table with a monotonous rhythm. "I have no quarrel with the jury. You know that."

"Or the judge's blast at them either?"

"That's right."

"Then you think the jury did a bum job?"

"That's right."

I leaned on my arms and watched him across the table. "Why do you think the jury turned in that verdict?"

The frown came back across his face again. "I don't know."

"Then guess."

His eyes crawled up my arm until they were searching mine. "You had a good lawyer, Regan. He pulled out all the stops. Despite every piece of incontrovertible evidence to the contrary, the jury couldn't figure you as gunning down Marcus. They chose to disbelieve four sober, blue ribbon eyewitnesses, a ballistics expert, a fingerprint expert, a lab report on the extent of your sobriety and a few other facts like a paraffin test and a cab driver's sworn statement that he took you roaring drunk from a bar to Marcus' house sounding off that you were going to kill the guy for getting you booted off the force. Just great, isn't it?"

"You forgot something, Jerry," I told him.

"Like what?"

"Like maybe they believed my side was the right one."

Cold cynicism was in the set of his mouth. "Sure. Like they really believed you didn't know a thing from the middle of your big drunk until you woke up in a cell a day and a half later. Sorry, Regan, but there's no logic in it. I think the jury decided the thing on the obtuse moral factors. Marcus was a big time hood. He had several previous convictions, had been tried and acquitted twice on murder charges, had been accused of being important in the drug traffic and at the time of his death was about to appear in court on tax evasion charges. Somehow, using that line of reasoning, twelve supposedly intelligent persons decided you were really a white knight after all and that the dragon really needed killing and you were sent back to the round table with a clean bill of health."

"Okay, Jerry, think it out any way you like. Only tell me this. Do you really think I knocked him off?"

"I think this, Regan. You could have. You're capable of it. It wouldn't surprise me if you did. Not even a little bit."

"All right, one more question. Do you think I took a bundle from Marcus to suppress evidence?"

The scowl left his face all at once. "If I did I wouldn't be talking to you now." He rapped the table with the flat of his hand. "But you're still poison until after the investigation."

"Investigation my neck! They going to call Marcus back as a witness? All they had was his complaint and five lousy grand your partner said he found in my room."

Nolan said quietly, "He found it there."

"Who cares. It was a plant. You know what I'm going to do, Jerry? I'm going to claim that bundle. If they can't prove it was Marcus' dough and I grafted it they're going to hand it back on a platter. One way or another I'm going to shove something up somebody."

Jerry fingered a pack of butts from his pocket and tapped one out on his hand. "You come all the way here to tell me this?"

"Not exactly." I held out a match to his cigarette. "I was

framed somehow. Real neat job. I don't know why or how, but I was framed."

"So's every con in Sing."

"But they're not outside to prove it."

"Go on."

"I'm going into this one, kiddo. Somebody's going to wind up big and dead."

"You're not a cop now, Regan."

"You are."

"And right now I'm not shooting anybody. You're crazy man. You're all gone. Four months in detention and you're all gone. What kind of notion have you got in your head that you're going out and shoot up somebody? That's hop talk, guy."

I grinned at him. "Jer . . . somebody's dead already. Marcus. Somebody framed me for the kill and a murderer is running around loose."

"The department will take care of that."

"Uh-uh. They just tab me for a lucky killer, that's all. They won't be looking too far for somebody else."

"What do you want from me, Regan?"

"A little information, that's all. The details of the bit never came through the walls of my cell."

"Like what?"

"Later I'll think of things. Did the hack company replace the cabbie who drove me to Marcus' place?"

His mind clicked back, fastened on it, and he said, "Guy Rivera? No, he still works the stand outside the *Climax* where you got tanked up."

I looked at him, grinned a little bigger and stood up.

Nolan said puzzledly, "That all?"

"For now. Tell Argenio I said hello."

Jerry glanced past me and a heavy voice with a snarl in it said, "Don't bother. Just keep walking."

I kept some of the grin on for Al, a nice toothy grin, and said, "Hi, slob."

The muscles along his jaws and neck jumped, but that was all. "You want me to move you on out, Regan?"

I was feeling too damn good and it showed. I said, "Remember the last time you tried it?"

His neck twitched again and he didn't say anything, but I knew he remembered all right. I waited long enough so he could have time to try once more if he felt like it, and when he didn't I said so-long to Jerry and walked out.

I got off the Seventh Avenue subway at Sheridan Square and went up into the rain again. The cleanness was gone now and the thick drizzle seemed to hold in all the wild smells of a city that had run hard all day. The streets had a greasy appearance, barely able to reflect the few lights still flashing along the Village at this hour. I turned my collar up, then cut across the street and headed down toward the *Climax*.

In its day it had been a flash spot and the histories of two great trumpets and the world's hottest sax had begun right here. But now all were dead, and on the relics the tourists had built legends and a purpose in keeping a gaudy gin mill operating.

I walked past it to the cab stand at the corner where three hacks edged the curb patiently and nudged the driver in the first one awake. He came to with a sleepy grin and started to reach back to open the door.

"Thanks anyway," I said, "but I'm looking for Guy Rivera. He here?"

He sat up and pawed at his eyes. "Guy? Oh . . . yeah." He waggled his thumb over his shoulder. "The last one down. Little feller."

I slipped a buck in his hand. "Here, go back to sleep." He grinned back and tucked the bill in his shirt pocket.

Guy Rivera had his head down reading the pink edition of a tabloid by the map light under the dash. I said, "Rivera . . ." and his head jerked up. He squinted, trying to see my face.

"Yeah?"

I moved into the light and when he saw me little concentric arcs grew at the corners of his mouth. "Listen, Mr. Regan . . ."

"Don't get nervous, Guy. I'm not on your back. Mind if I sit in the cab?"

He shook his head, but his mouth stayed tight. I opened the door, climbed in and leaned back against the seat.

I said, "You know why I'm here?"

His tongue wet his lips down and he coughed into his hand. "Look, you know what I said at the trial. So I said it and that's it. What'd I do?"

"You were on the stand no more than ten minutes, Rivera. You made a statement of fact that you picked me up here, drove me to Marcus' place and all the while I rambled on about killing somebody. You weren't even cross-examined."

Rivera coughed again and nodded jerkily. "And it's the truth. What'd you think I could say. Hell, Mr. Regan, why're you picking on me, now. You got off. You . . ."

"I said I wasn't on your back."

"Then whatta you want from me?"

"A couple of minor things that never came out at the trial. Let's ask them now."

"Sure."

"You remember everything that happened?"

"How you expect me to forget? Here I drive you out so you can . . ."

"Drop it. Let's start at the beginning. Where were you when I got in the cab?"

"In the front spot. Chick and Dooley were right behind me."

"And I came out and got in the cab?"

"Yeah."

"I was supposed to have been pretty drunk."

He fidgeted in his seat and tugged at the shift lever. "Well, you got in. The place was closing up. You weren't the only rum dum coming out."

"Think hard, Guy. Who put me in the cab?"

"How do I know! Hell, you know how it is. Drunks all over the place. Somebody gives them an arm in. All the time it happens."

"I never get that soused, friend. Who was doing the favors?"

He shoved the lever away from him and twisted around. Worry and fright were stark things that drew thin lines down the lean cheeks and a fine bead of sweat wet his forehead. "I don't want to make trouble, Mr. Regan."

"You won't."

"Well . . . they didn't let me say much at the trial. Just asked a few questions. But when . . . that . . . happened I kept thinking about it, me being so close to it. Hell, I could even have stopped it if I knowed. You come out of there with a bunch of people, but some broad stuffed you in the cab."

"Broad?"

"Yeah. Now I didn't see her face good because I wasn't looking, see? But she was a redhead. Looked real. Only thing I remember is her pocketbook. I thought it was binoculars first, then she opens it and drags out a pack of smokes so I knows it's her pocketbook. Big letter B in gold on one side. While you're getting in she asks you if you still want to see-some-rat-and-what-was-his-name. That's when you started mumbling about Leo Marcus and how you'd kill 'im. She asks where he lived and you told me. Top of High Street, you said. Big brick house. She made you pay in advance with a fin so I took you there, all the time talking about this Marcus."

"How come you didn't refuse the fare, Guy?"

"Ah, it was drunk talk, Mr. Regan. You know how it is. Guys talking to themselves. Sometimes it's worse if you refuse. Then there's real trouble. Anyway, I took you there."

"Right to the door?"

Rivera made a face. "Naw. To the curb. You got out and just stood there. That's when I drove away."

"I was in pretty bad shape?"

"I've seen worse. Not often, though."

I said, "Rivera . . . there's a steep flight of stone steps going up to Marcus' front door. You think I could have made it?"

He squinched up his face again and hunched uncomfortably. "Maybe you weren't so bad off, after all. Sometimes . . ."

"I didn't ask that."

For a few seconds he didn't say anything, then quietly, "No." He swiveled around in his seat and gave me a searching look. "You know what's got me, Mr. Regan?"

"What?"

"I'd say you were so stiff you couldn't see to you-know-what. How you could pump six slugs into a guy's head is beyond me."

"It's beyond me too."

"Whatcha going to do now, Mr. Regan?"

"Find the girl."

"I'm gonna tell you something."

"What?"

"I ain't never seen her again."

"You said you didn't see her face."

"I know, but all the redheads I seen so far around the joint I know. This one I didn't know. See?"

"You'll keep looking?"

"Sure. So long as there's no trouble."

"You won't get bothered." I reached for a bill in my pocket and he waved it off.

"This is for friends, Mr. Regan."

"Okay. If you want me leave a call at Donninger's. You know where it is?"

"I know."

"And thanks, Rivera."

"Anytime."

*   *   *

The bartender at the *Climax* wore a stitched nameplate that read "RALPH" in red caps on his white mess jacket, a busy little guy with all the touches of a long time pro. He didn't see me come in, but rather felt my presence behind him and turned with a "What'll you have?" smile.

It lasted only a second, then it was gone and he nodded coolly and said, "Evening, Mr. Regan."

"Hello, Ralph." He waited for my order. "Tall ginger," I told him.

He set it up, his eyes wary, and when he took my change started to turn away.

"Come here, buddy."

He turned around, frowning. "I got nothing to say to you, pal. Nothing. Just keep off me, or I'll call in for a prowl car."

I looked at him for a long time. Too long for him. He almost dropped a glass he was wiping. "That could be a mistake, buddy."

He worked his mouth, then muttered softly, "Okay, whatta ya want?"

"Talk."

"You already heard everything I got to say."

"Somebody else was asking the questions."

"Well I got nothing else . . ."

I cut him off. "Let's say I want an opinion, huh?"

Ralph glanced around nervously, but nobody else was at the bar. "Like what?"

"You remember everything that night I was here?"

He shrugged and scowled. "I remember you getting stoned."

"Not quite."

"Whatta ya mean! I see you . . ."

"You saw me stoned, not *getting* stoned. There's a difference. You remember what you served me at the bar here?"

"Sure. You had a couple rye and gingers. Hell, I knew who you were then from your pictures in the papers."

"Two drinks didn't stone me, friend. I came in here sober, remember?"

Ralph didn't like what I was getting at a bit.

I said, "You testified I was drinking here for about three hours until the place closed up. But all you actually saw me have was two drinks."

"Listen, Mr. Regan, I work drunks. When I see a drunk I know . . ."

"How'd I get so drunk, buddy?"

Suddenly his face got red and tight lines stood out in his neck. His breath came out in a hiss. "If you think I slipped you a mickey, pal, you're crazy. Real crazy. You . . ."

"I went back to a table," I said softly. "I was sitting with Stan The Pencil. I was asking questions and he was able to answer some. He took me to another table and introduced me to a couple of local characters . . ."

"You was with Popeye Lewis and Edna Rells. Artists. I can . . ."

"I know who they are, friend." I paused, then: "Who waited on that table?"

"Spud. That's his section. But don't think he fed you anything, Mr. Regan. That old man has been here ten years and

90

worked this neighborhood all his life. He's square all the way."

I grinned at his loyalty. It seemed out of place in a gin mill. "Just curious, Ralph. Just curious. You remember anything about a redhead who joined the table?"

He shrugged. "Who looks at redheads? Here they're a dime a dozen."

"One helped me into the cab. She was a stranger here."

"If she didn't drink at the bar, then I don't remember her."

"Call Spud over."

He shook his head, annoyed at the whole routine, but walked to the end of the bar, scanned the back room, then waved. A minute later a grey-haired waiter in a tired tux worn thin from too many pressings came in, smiled and waited patiently for a complaint or compliment. On a second studied look he recognized me and glanced to Ralph for an explanation. The bartender shrugged and pointed his thumb at me.

"You remember me, Spud?"

He nodded. "Yessir."

"You remember the party that night?"

He made a small gesture with his shoulders. "I remember some. I had a party at every table that night."

"But you've had reason to remember this party, Spud. With all the publicity and having it start right here I bet you've thought back on it plenty of times."

When I stopped and waited he shuffled his feet and fidgeted. "I gave it some thought," he finally admitted.

"Who was at the party?"

He stared at me blankly a moment, thinking. "Popeye, Edna, then Miles Henry came in with them two pictures of Popeye's that the boss bought and then a lot of people came over to look at the paintings."

"I remember the art work," I said. "Seems to me that's about the last I remember."

The old man didn't believe me at all. His eyes tightened at the corners and his face reflected the cynicism the years had built up.

I said, "Do you remember me being drunk or sober then?"

"Mister," he said, "I wasn't paying attention to anybody being either way. In this business nobody ever gets more sober with each drink, they only get more drunk. I watched it happen but I didn't pay attention to it, otherwise when I see pictures of drunks smashing up people with their cars or shooting their kids in bed I'd maybe start drinking myself because it's partly my fault. So for you, I don't remember anything. Later on I noticed you all shook up because you were a quiet drunk and at that stage them's the kind to watch out for because the fuse was lit and with another few you'd be roaring. I've had some of 'em go for me when they were like that and now I watch for it. Sure I remember you then, and later too because you were crocked like hell and couldn't hardly walk and everybody was laughing at you."

It was quite a speech. I ran over it in my mind before I asked him, "Who was everybody?"

Again I got that noncommittal shrug. "There was a crowd at the table then."

"You know them?"

"Nope. Stan The Pencil had gone to make book in the other joints and Popeye and Edna stayed with the boss the rest of the night. You had a bunch of strangers with you. That's the way it goes here. Parties. Always parties."

"Who footed the bill?"

"You paid by rounds. Everybody had money on the table in front of them. You too."

"Remember a redhead at the party? She carried a handbag that was shaped like a binocular case."

"Sure," he said.

I didn't interrupt him. I let him reach for it himself. "A big beautiful job and she was all over you. She got you outa here when we closed up."

Inside my chest I felt all tight and my mouth had a dry feel. Quietly, I said, "Who was she?"

Then the tightness turned into an inaudible curse. Because he gave me that shrug again and said, "I don't know. Just some broad."

I fished four bucks out of my pocket and split it between the two of them. "Thanks. If you see her around, give me a call. I'm in the book."

Ralph just nodded. Spud looked thoughtful a moment, fingered the two bucks in his hand, then looked at me purposefully. "Mr. Regan . . ."

"What?"

"I don't think you could've bumped that guy."

"Why not?"

"All my life I worked drunks. I know what they can do. You couldn't see to bump anybody that night."

"That's what I tried to tell them, Spud."

He had something else to say but didn't quite know how to get it out. Finally he said, "I've known plenty of crooked cops, Mr. Regan. I hated their guts."

"Go on."

"Did you take a payoff from Marcus?"

"No. That was a framed job."

The grin on Spud's face was a friendly one.

"What did you expect me to say, anyway?"

92

"I could've told if you were lying, Mr. Regan. I'll let you know if I see her again."

You find friends in funny places, I thought. I watched him leave, then walked outside and down the subway where I caught a train for my apartment.

CHAPTER TWO

GEORGE LUCAS grew up on the same street I did and was all set to break into the mob when he took time out to count the cost and figured it too high. Instead, he worked his way through school and became a criminal-law lawyer. But he still looked like a crook and half the time he acted like one. His record in court was imposing. He could out-shyster the shysters anytime and if he could stick a needle up the DA.'s tail he'd take the case free.

When I walked into his office he grinned crookedly and said, "I had an idea you'd be around."

"Why?"

"I don't know, Regan. It was just a feeling. You did okay in court. How could you afford Selkirk and Selkirk? That's big time."

I sat down and tossed my hat on his desk. "They came free, Georgie. Monty Selkirk figured he owed me a favor. I let him pay it back."

"You got his kid off the hook one time, didn't you?"

I shrugged. "He wasn't involved. It was a phoney blackmail attempt."

"Good to have buddies like that. Always have something working for you that way." He flipped open a box of cigars, offered me one and when I said no, lit up himself. "So what's with you today, Patrick?"

"Something up your alley."

"Let's have it."

"You familiar with my case?"

"Everything, boy. It's home town news, you know."

"Yeah." I leaned back and stuck out my feet. "Well, just to review you, I was assigned to the Leo Marcus thing. We'd picked up a rumble that he was back in the extortion racket among other things."

George nodded and sucked on the cigar. "I heard about it. He was getting up there."

"He *was* there, friend. He ran the organizational operation along the Atlantic coast from New York to the toe of Florida. He set up a string of motels with organization money for one thing, used each unit as a local headquarters and clearing house and did it so nice and legally he couldn't be touched."

"Smart," George said. "The new method. Keep it legal."

"He didn't quite make it. I had a tipoff that would have wrapped up the entire deal. It took eight weeks, but I had a dossier on Leo Marcus complete with incriminating evidence that would have blown the operation sky high. Just before the end of the investigation I met with two of the commissioners at a midtown hotel so they could pave the way for us to hit the operation without tipping off the papers. That night they saw what I had and knew what it meant."

"That was your mistake, hey, kiddo?"

I nodded. "That was it. They knew I had it and when I couldn't produce it again I was cooked. That made the money plant look real."

George pointed with the cigar. "About the loot . . ."

I laughed at him. He still sounded Brooklyn. "The loot, friend, was five lousy G's. An anonymous call to HQ said I sold out and Argenio hit my flat where he found a package of fifty one-hundred-dollar bills supposedly hidden in my closet. I was held, I couldn't come up with my file and couldn't account for the cash. Open and shut."

"Just like that?"

"That's the size of it."

"They didn't take your departmental record into consideration?"

"Give them a break. They tried. I have a lot of friends around, George."

"You're not lacking in enemies, either. So go."

I went. "I probably could have stood off the charges. The second mistake was in getting mad."

"You always were like that, Patrick. Even when you were a little kid I used to tell you to take it easy. Think you'd listen? Hell, no."

"So I wanted to know who put the finger on me. It came down through Marcus, but I wanted to know who passed the word. I was working the stoolies when I got tagged."

"Like how?"

"Like I was slipped a mickey and steered out to Marcus' place."

"And there it ends," he said around his cigar.

I nodded.

"You were lucky," he told me. "One thing, you just can't always figure a jury. You talked it up enough before Marcus got killed. You know how many guys . . . cops yet, heard you say you'd put so many holes in him he'd look like a screen door?"

"That was talk. You know damn well how it goes."

"Sure, but it got done. Man, six shots in the kisser that knocked him kicking into a fireplace so that he's half cremated before they find you both." He leaned back in his chair, blowing smoke up toward the ceiling. "Until they found the finger that was shot off him they weren't even sure it was Marcus. Of course, the dentist they ran down made it positive, but for a while they were shook. Hell, you . . . if it *was* you . . . did everybody a big favor. The cops should be happy."

"It wasn't me."

"Your gun. Your prints. Paraffin test. You're there out drunk. You made threats. You had a great motive. It's pretty strong, Patrick."

"Was pretty strong, remember?"

He grinned and nodded. "Selkirk's a good lawyer. So what do you want from me?"

"My five grand. It was impounded. There might be a technicality or two involved, but since I have the name, I want the game. That five G's Argenio found is mine, right?"

George's face got real bright. "An interesting thought, Patrick. You played the ponies, hit a goodie, now spill out the tax and it's yours. I think it can be arranged."

"Then arrange it. Whoever planted that loot is financing his own funeral."

He leaned forward, the concern on his face showing in the tight lines around his mouth. "This might louse you up in the department."

"The hell with 'em. They can't do anything but clear me. But I want that cash."

"Sure, Patrick, I'll get it for you. Anything else?"

"Yeah, one thing. Represent me at the departmental trial."

"Sure, but what about meanwhile?"

"You know me, Georgie boy. I'm nobody's slob."

"That's what I'm afraid of. You packing a rod?"

"Not at the moment."

"Later?"

"If I have to."

"Like I said," he repeated. "What about meanwhile?"

"I want my badge back. They'll probably try to shuffle me off to some obscure division, so make a deal. I'll keep nice and clean and out of everybody's way. Otherwise I'll really raise a stink. They'll know what I'm talking about."

"So do I, kid. The picture's clear. You're just asking for a bucketful of trouble and an early death."

"Didn't I always?"

"You did. That you did. You're such a damn big target it's a wonder you ever stayed alive this long."

I picked my hat off his desk and slid it on. "Take care of me, Georgie boy."

"Just like the old days," he said.

I nodded. "So now I got a mouthpiece. Fine comedown for a cop." I grinned at him. "Just like the old days."

*   *   *

Jerry Nolan always ate Saturday lunches at Vinnie's. The menu was wop clam chowder with all the breadsticks you could eat stacked up like cordwood in the middle of the table. Vinnie automatically dished up a plate for me and had it at the table as soon as I sat down. When I said hello he nodded, the reserve plain on his face. I was something he wasn't used to. Ordinarily everything would be black or white, but now something was grey and he wasn't used to it.

"You're taking a long time," I finally said to him.

He paused, a half a breadstick heavy with butter halfway to his mouth. "What are you getting at?"

"You. Your damn insistence upon the letter of the law all the way. By now you should figure yourself for a sanctimonious bastard in a departmental sense."

His face tightened and he bit into the breadstick, waiting.

"The law, buddy," I said. "It proved me innocent. Remember? You're the one always sounding off about the sanctity of the law. Now the law has acted. I'm clean. Come off it. Like you tell everybody else, don't figure yourself bigger than the law so that when the law acts you refuse to accept the verdict."

His neck reddened and he bent his face toward his plate. His eyes flicked up momentarily and he nodded, trying to conceal a self-conscious smile.

"Okay."

That's all he said, and I knew everything was all right again. Nolan was a funny one, a hell of a tough cop, but square all the way. His hatred for hoods was a terrible passion but nothing compared to the way he felt about crooked cops. He had had a hard time swallowing the thing that had happened to me, but now it was dead and buried.

I said, "I picked up something."

"New?"

"To me, anyway. A redhead helped me into a cab that night."

"She wasn't there when you got out. You took that ride alone," he reminded me. He spooned his chowder up again, then: "You weren't followed, either. I questioned Rivera about that myself. He was positive."

"The redhead set up the address. Damn it, I had been mouthing off about Marcus and she had me driven there."

With a patient gesture he put his spoon down and wiped his mouth. "I know, Regan. I heard it all. I'm not stupid. I checked out everything that night personally. I didn't pass any of it on because there was nothing conclusive. It's pretty typical of people who have been drinking to help another drunk into a cab. Nobody makes sense. Everybody's at the ha ha stage. The driver gets paid and goes along with things. Any cabbie will drop a drunk off at an address. He won't get wrapped up over it."

"This didn't come out at the trial."

"I said it was inconclusive. You had enough against you. I didn't have to make it any worse."

"Thanks."

"My pleasure."

"You overlooked one thing."

"Now I know."

"All right, tell it to me," I said.

"You were slipped a mickey sometime that night."

"Thanks for realizing it. You know why?"

"Sure. So you could kill off Marcus."

I shook my head. "You know damn well that would be a stupid trick. I was too far gone to do anything. I was set up for a conviction and you know it. Anybody that drunk would have the cops asking questions long before a jury would."

Nolan leaned back in his seat and reached for his cigarettes. When he had one lit he said, "You know the ingredients in a mickey?"

I nodded. "Sure. Generally chloral hydrate. For the knockout kind, anyway."

"That's right. But the restriction on its use is that it knocks you out or doesn't knock you out. If you went under you wouldn't be able to act of your own volition. However, during the war the Germans came up with a new one. A simple formula change brought the desired results, but when certain initial effects had worn off, the subject had physical action without mental control and no later recollection."

A small fire started deep in my belly. "Go on."

"It was called Sentol. It allowed a person to come out of a stupor, perform an act, then go back into a stupor again."

"This didn't come out at the trial," I said coldly.

"I realize that. Again, it was inconclusive. When you were found you were given the usual balloon test for drunks. The percentage was against you. The kind of a dosage you could possibly . . . and I said *possibly* . . . have been given, would have allowed you to drink enough to genuinely get drunk, at least enough to go past the critical percentage point in your blood. By all known tests, you were chemically drunk."

"So why this sudden slant?"

"Ted Marker, up in the lab, is probably only one of the few familiar with Sentol. Occasionally he tests for it. Unfortunately, too much time had passed for a positive result, but what he found was curious."

"Being curious and uncovering facts are pretty far apart."

"Sure, but that's as far as he got. The analysis showed a couple of indications of the presence of Sentol. It was a bare possibility."

Then I realized just how far out on a limb they had gone for me. In one way I could have been victimized by that damn drug, but just as surely I could have killed Marcus.

He let it sink in, then went on. "Sentol, from what Ted knows about it, was originally called a 'conscience remover.' Properly administered, it allowed you to fulfill the desires of the primary passions like love or hate or fear. In your case it would be hatred. You wanted to kill Marcus so the drug removed any restrictions on you for doing so."

"That is," I said, "if it was administered."

"Of course."

"Now things are getting a little too obvious, aren't they?"

Nolan shrugged, dragged in deeply on his cigarette, letting out the smoke in a controlled grey stream. "There are only two possibilities. One . . . you killed him. Two . . . somebody else did and arranged very elaborately for you to be the patsy."

"That makes me pretty important."

For a few moments Jerry sat there studying the ash on his cigarette, then he turned those cold eyes on me and said, "Just what did you have on Marcus?"

His tone was a patient one. Waiting was nothing new to him at all. I said, "You remember when I was assigned to Marcus?"

He nodded and pulled on the smoke again. "I knew that you had been assigned, but not the nature of the deal."

"Orders came from the top. Only six people knew that I was to concentrate on Marcus. I could work in my own way and nobody was over me directing the operation. There was a limited fund made available so I could buy information if necessary and if I had to work outside normal jurisdiction I was guaranteed quick cooperation with other departments. It was set up pretty much like with the Parker kidnapper and the Small-Greenblatt spy thing."

"I remember them both."

"In brief, Leo Marcus' operation was the result of the heat

put on the Syndicate ever since the Apalachin raid. The Syndicate couldn't function as a unit and rather than have it fall apart into fragments that would be difficult to reassemble later, they set it up into sections that would operate individually until they were ready to bring them back under one head again.

"Marcus had the choicest bit. He had the money spots from New York to Miami and you know how he ran them. He was a strong-arm character right out of the Capone books but shrewd enough not to get caught. My opinion is that he was the most vicious hood the Syndicate ever had and he didn't get knocked off any too soon.

"Anyway, I waited him out. I had the law of averages working for me. Along the line he made a couple of mistakes and before he found out about them and covered up, I found out about them and had him cold."

"For instance," Jerry prompted.

"He killed a kid in a drive-in down in Georgia. He was drunk and there was a girl involved. He fractured the guy's skull with a billy and the girl ran off in a panic. Leo's companion in the car, a small-time local hood working for him, did Leo a favor and found the broad and scared her off. I found the hood. It didn't take much to persuade him that Leo didn't like live witnesses to a murder and he talked up nicely. He even went further . . . he gave me the sap Leo had used on the kid complete with prints, the kid's blood and hair particles, signed a statement and promised to testify at the trial, although with the evidence at hand it wasn't necessary. He was held in the local jail, word spread fast, and the next day he was dead of food poisoning with nobody able to explain how. But like I said, his death wasn't quite necessary."

"So you had to go," Nolan said.

"Something like that. Or else they had to get the information I had."

"Why didn't you turn it in while you had it?"

"Because the deal wasn't set up that way. The commissioners knew it and didn't ask for it. The procedure had already been established. They just saw what I had, that's all. That was enough."

"What did you have on the operation?"

"In general, a breakdown of Atlantic system. Leo's unit owned and operated a string of motels, all nice and legally complicated. Each place was a drop where the mob did business. What facts I had on individuals weren't worth pressing. That would come later. The primary job was to outline the operation so a team could move in for the big kill later."

"And now it's gone," Nolan said dryly.

I shrugged. "I could duplicate it from memory, but what good would it do. By now the system has changed completely. The only real bit then was the murder evidence that would have sent Marcus to the hot squat."

He snubbed the cigarette out and waved to Vinnie for more coffee. "The Brotherhood is getting pretty nervous. Their big wheels aren't supposed to be getting messed up in two-bit kills."

"It happens," I said.

"But only once, Regan. They get touchy about those things. Nobody is indispensable. If a wheel is likely to make trouble for the mob, then out he goes. Look what happened to Dutch Schultz when they thought he was going to knock off Dewey."

I sipped at the coffee, staring at him across the cup. "I know. I was thinking about that. And like the man said, therein lies the puzzle."

Nolan frowned and didn't answer me.

"Never before did they bother to get so damn elaborate about it. Always it was just a few rounds from a chopper."

He put his cup down and wiped at his mouth. "Sometimes it's worth while, especially if they got a tailor-made patsy like you seemed to be." He grinned when he saw my mouth go tight and added, "Now what do you want from me? You didn't come here to rehash most of what I already knew."

"Who tipped Argenio?" I said.

He seemed to stiffen under his coat and finely drawn lines showed at the corners of his eyes. When he looked at me it was with annoyance. "You know anonymous tips, Regan."

"Sure, but not on a cop with a good record." I waited a second then said, "Why the sudden push?"

He nodded soberly and sat back, still not liking the talk. "This is under the hat, kid. The tip was made to our office. Argenio took it, called the commissioner because the tipster said to do it, and the commish in person directed Argenio to get to your place."

"The call go through the switchboard?"

"That's right, but it wasn't monitored. It came in at eleven-ten p.m., and Jackson, who was on the PBX, had too many calls going to monitor any single one."

"Neat, wasn't it?" I asked him.

"Let's say effective."

I sprung it on him quickly. "What do you think of Argenio?"

He didn't like it. His face showed as much. "Fourteen years on the force, he did all right. He has three commendations."

"I have twelve. That wasn't the question."

Nolan leaned forward, his hands gripping the edge of the table. His voice was quiet, but had a hard edge. "Look . . . he's my partner and has been for two years. He's covered me in a lot of tight places plenty of times. What do you expect me to say?"

"That's what any partner is supposed to do. For all those heroics he draws a regular wage. Now answer the question."

I saw his fingers relax and the indecision come into his eyes. "I don't know. He's a hard apple. He's hard on everybody and he's harder on himself. You tangled with him once."

"I knocked his damn ass off," I said.

"Okay. He's strange, let's say."

"Susceptible to a bribe?"

"Plainly, no. I know that he was offered some big loot, but he wouldn't touch it."

"You don't like him, though, do you?"

"No," Jerry said, "I don't like him. Nevertheless, that doesn't change matters. He's a damn good cop with nothing against him and there are others that I feel the same about so an opinion like mine isn't worth anything. What are you getting at, anyway?"

"He seemed to move pretty fast, busting into my apartment to follow up an anonymous tip."

"He was ordered to."

"I could have been contacted. I wasn't that hard to find."

"The stuff was gone and he found five grand in unexplained dough."

"He didn't figure a plant?"

"Damn it, Regan, we all figured a plant. It was too pat. Maybe we could have done something if you didn't go off on a bat and . . ." He paused, shook his head and flipped another butt out of his pack.

I said softly, "You'll keep looking around?"

He nodded, lighting the cigarette. "I'll look around."

I finished my coffee and climbed out of the booth. When I reached for the check Nolan waved me off, his face still impassive. I said, "If you want me, leave a call at Donninger's."

His mind closed on the name, remembering the phone number from other contacts we had made there. "What will you be doing?" His voice was the wrong tone. It wasn't cop to cop any more.

I said, "Something new has been added, remember?"

"Oh?"

"Somebody had to take Marcus' place."

* * *

I wasted the day doing legwork around some of the old places, but things weren't the same any more. In a way I was still a cop, but a cop under suspension isn't quite a cop and there was more lip than talk. I let it go for a while and the wise guys knew what it meant. If the suspension didn't stick I'd be back to talk to them again and there were going to be some sore faces around. To people like that you talk better with your hands than your mouth. A few still had impressions of the last time we had to talk and rattled off some, but not enough to steer me onto a direct line.

Time. It all took time. You don't go after the big ones overnight. I let it be known around that I was still looking and those who saw my face knew just how badly I wanted somebody. They knew what would happen when I found that somebody and they knew that I wasn't going to stop looking for anything or anybody.

The word would go around and nobody would like it a bit, but there wasn't a thing they could do about it at all. Except one thing.

Somebody could make sure I got killed.

When I got home I was tired and dirty and needed a shave. I climbed under the shower and soaked the dirt and sweat off, shaved without drying down, then wrapped a towel around me and went outside to the kitchen for a cold beer and a sandwich.

For a while I stood there eating, watching the traffic go by on the street below. For a change it was a quiet evening. Before the night was over the chart said there would be from nine to fifteen unexplained deaths, three murders of passion, several hundred cuttings and probably a dozen nice clean shootings with the persons involved apprehended before morning. Rapes, muggings, burglaries numerous, but unnumbered on the chart.

What the chart didn't show was the subtle creeping thing that was the soft kill. Voters who supported corruption and taxpayers who paid for it. Out there in the evening the big ones who constituted the royalty of vice were getting dressed to preside over their dominions. The serfs would pay hidden tribute by name dropping. Their direct overlords would pay direct tribute in different ways. In a way, everybody paid a tribute and if you didn't like it there was a place to put it. You know.

Whoredom was dead in the city, the papers said. The administration had announced very solemnly that aside from those pursuing the world's oldest profession along the street and an occasional call girl working limited operations, generally apprehended, that organized whoredom was dead, dead, dead.

Why didn't someone tell them about Madison Avenue's Miss Mad? She published a brochure of her wares and for a thousand bucks you got pictures and backgrounds of three hundred and seven of her "models." Her name was Madaline Stumper . . . Miss Mad to the trade . . . and she lived in the good seventies with a million a year coming in. She paid off half that million to the Brotherhood and another quarter of it to certain ones in the city. But what the hell, anybody can live on a quarter million a year, can't they?

For five years the bright boys have been trying to track down the marijuana traffic and make feeble excuses when they can't ring the bell. Hell, everybody close enough to the business knows about Hymie Reeves seeding out abandoned farms in Orange County with the stuff and going in at the right time to harvest it. If a cow gets drunk on the loco weed the farmers generally attribute it to "fallen apples" and let the cow sober up. If somebody spots it growing it gets chopped down in a burst of civic pride and glory with pictures in the local papers. If nobody sees it grow, Hymie comes in at the right time with a pickup and harvests it out on a dark night and makes a bundle. It's only a weed. No cultivating. No care. It mixes with the sumac, grows like crazy and is an invitation to ride the horse that comes later. Great. Just great.

And on the waterfront the big H comes in like on a pneumatic tube in a department store and so long as the right people get paid hardly anything gets tipped. The fraction of all the stuff that gets stopped by the cops is really only a diversionary tactic to satisfy an understaffed agency and satiate the press. But the tips are for real and the boys go in. They pick up the stuff and it's worth the raid, but meanwhile a hundred times as much goes though and what's lost gets written off just like in business.

The soft kill. Like a gorgeous, wonderful, but syphilitic whore.

Behind me the phone rang and I snapped out of all the things I had been thinking. I put the beer down and picked it up. The voice on the other end said, "Mr. Regan? This Mr. Regan?"

I couldn't place it at first. "This is Regan."

"I told you I'd call, Mr. Regan. This is Spud, from the *Climax*, remember?"

"Oh, sure, Spud, what's up?"

"I found the redhead, Mr. Regan. Rivera backs me up on it."

Across the room from me there was a mirror and when I looked into it I was grinning. There was no reason to grin at all and looking at the reflection was a peculiar thing. I was grinning, but I couldn't feel it on my face at all.

I said, "Where, Spud," and tried to keep the excitement out of my voice.

"Tonight's paper," he said easily. "Two pictures in the *News*. Front and page three. She was found dead in the river. The cops say an apparent suicide."

Suddenly the hot feeling in my gut went away and left a tightness and when I looked back in the mirror I wasn't smiling any more at all.

I said, "Thanks, Spud."

And he told me, "My pleasure, Mr. Regan. I hope you can still do what you have to do."

"I will," I said, and hung up.

CHAPTER THREE

THE front page was a body shot over a caption showing the police launch in the background and a pair of cops laying out the still wet figure of a woman. The story inside was accompanied by a full-face photo of a lovely girl in her late twenties with soft, flowing hair curling down around her shoulders highlighting a sensual, full-lipped smile. The picture was one taken from a wallet she had in her suit jacket and the brief news account stated that she was identified as Mildred Swiss from her Social Security card and driver's license. No cause was given for the drowning, but the police suspected suicide and were checking all Missing Persons reports and looking for the next of kin.

I studied the face again, closer this time. The photo was more than a simple snapshot. The clarity was unusual and the posture too professional for an amateur job. And there was that thing about her mouth and the provocative slant to her eyes.

Not everybody was riding my back. Van Reeves in the records section and I had had too many contacts for him to pull out the stops and hedge on things like this. One time he had been caught in a trap too and knew what it was like. He was glad to hear from me and told me so.

I said, "Favor, Van."

"Listening."

"A girl was fished out of the river last night. Redhead named Mildred Swiss."

"Yeah, I saw it."

"Any request on her I.D. come through your department?"

"Not yet. Should it?"

"Eventually. They probably sent her prints directly to Washington, but see if she was listed as a cabaret performer in the city. She looks the type."

"Will do. Can you hold on?"

"Sure."

Van didn't take long. He came back, picked up the phone and I could hear him rustling sheets of paper in his hand. "Got it, Regan. She's a naturalized citizen of Polish origin with an unpronounceable last name. Last address is in the Fifties, but it won't do you any good because they tore all that section down for a new hotel and she never renewed. Parents deceased, no listed relatives."

"Who sponsored her into the country?"

"Parents. Home in Linden, New Jersey, where they died. Looks like they got here during the war and sent for her later. I'll have to pass this on."

"Anything in the other files?"

"No criminal record in this city. Something may turn up somewhere else. What are you thinking of?"

"She's a type, Van."

"Hunch or you know?"

"Just one of those things. Thanks."

"No trouble. Glad you put me on it. Call anytime."

"It's nice to know you still have friends," I said.

"Nuts. You'd be surprised. Now you'll have more than ever."

"Sure," I told him sarcastically and hung up.

After so many years you begin to read the signs. You can see things in expressions and make the nuances of oblique fact channel themselves into paths nobody else would ever notice. It was part of being a cop and a part that nothing but experience and a tiny, ingrained feeling could give you.

Mildred Swiss looked like a type and her background had the little hooks you could hang certain probabilities on. She had steered me into a murder rap and now that it had come unglued, she was dead. Lucky coincidences just don't come that often. The laws of chance are too strange, too varied.

I grinned and sucked my breath through my teeth, knowing that someplace out there in the crosshatch pattern of the city somebody was sitting and waiting, guts churning with anxiety because I was loose and I'd be looking. He'd be playing a big game and the stakes were absolute.

There was no coming back from the dead.

That was the absolute.

* * *

She occupied a suite of offices that took up a corner of the fourth floor of the new Galton-Mead building on Madison Avenue, an exclusive address catering only to the finest tenants or those prepared to pay an exorbitant rental.

Each door bore the gold-lettered name, *Sturvesent Agency*, a respected firm that handled some of the highest fashion models in the business and worked with nothing but the leading magazines in the field. Six leading movie stars and a few dozen big TV names had come from the Sturvesent list.

So did a lot of others who never gained national prominence.

The Sturvesent Agency was a supplier of the fanciest call girls in town too.

A long time ago Madaline Stumper had started in a small way. Luck and diligent enterprise had gotten her to the top, but that curious quirk of nature that drew her into being a madam at nineteen had kept her in the sex business from then on, working at an executive level among the biggest business in the world, with friends in high places and an income that didn't show in the tax forms.

It was a cute operation. In this crazy world some said it merely filled a demand that would always be there, catered to accepted organizational procedures and was as much a part of business as the clients who requested the services of her stable.

One thing about Miss Mad. She ran both ends with identical and remarkable efficiency. She had never taken a fall, and although she had been questioned on several occasions, a battery of high-priced lawyers quashed the whole thing and had her loose in a matter of minutes. All the department ever got were a few leaks, a word here and there that was too second hand to process and an idea of what she was up to. No disgruntled customers ever registered a complaint and no amount of undercover work ever pointed a condemning finger her way.

I walked in to where the silver blonde was sitting behind a polished mahogany desk, a full-bodied woman in her early thirties with eyes that could pick you clean in seconds and tabulate before you crossed the thick nylon rug from the door.

Her smile was friendly, but there was a frigidity in her eyes that said she could smell gun oil on me and see the hole in my wallet where the badge used to be pinned. She said, "Yes?" Nothing more. It was enough.

"Tell Miss Mad I'd like to see her. Pat Regan."

Her eyebrows went up slowly, querulously, an unspoken challenge.

"We're old friends," I told her.

In a way we were. We had graduated from high school together and twice back in the neighborhood I had pulled a guy off her back who had been trying to make her the hard way and twice I had wound up bloody and sore.

Whatever was in my voice made a lie out of my grin. The receptionist wet her lips with the tip of her tongue and she didn't push the matter. She spun the dial of her phone, held the husher mouthpiece up close so I couldn't catch the conversation, then put it back and said, "Her secretary will be right out."

"Thanks," I nodded.

For five minutes I had time to watch the traffic. They came and went through the many doors, tall, emaciated women with necks that reminded me of what Mr. Guillotine thought of when he mechanized the chopping block. They all looked hungry, their cheekbones prominent, dresses and coats nipped in around hourglass waists, hair piled in the latest fashion and all flat chested as hell. Only a couple wore wedding rings and it was easy to see why. In bed it would be like having a few loose pipes aboard.

But not all of them were like that. Two happy, well-fed types came bouncing in, deliberately displaying a lot of flesh money-tailored in the kind of clothes that would turn any man inside out, pushed through the gate and went into one of the offices.

Before they came out the pert kid in the green dress tapped my arm and said, "This way, Mr. Regan."

We went through a long corridor behind the other rooms, then turned and she opened a door. I thanked her, stepped inside and looked across the room at the stunning sight of the woman I used to fight over and said, "Hello, Mad."

She was a composite of all the world's beauties until you reached her eyes, then you saw in the great depths of those almost-black orbs that matched the silky sheen of her hair the vast depths of a cavern that held an unknown life of their own.

Only for a second did they seem to fill up with what should have been there in the first place, then whatever it was receded a little . . . there, but not showing all the way. Her mouth was a flower that blossomed red, accented by the white of even teeth, and one corner had a tiny grin to it. "Regan. Well, well."

"It's been a long time."

"Not really. I've been reading about you."

"Hasn't everybody?"

Madaline Stumper stood up and held out her hand to me. No matter who she had working for the agency, they could never touch her. Her grip was firm and warm, mocking sin-

107

cerity in her hello. Beneath the black dress she was a woman of physical beauty rarely seen any more. High breasts that dared you with every curving line, taut stomach muscles that ebbed and flowed like a tide into generous thighs that held a fluid, hungry stance unknowingly deliberate, a gesture she had ever since she was a kid.

I let go her hand and dragged a chair up with my foot, waited until she sat down and slouched into it. "You're looking damn good, kid."

She let the grin go wide a moment. "What a choice of words. The other day the president of A.T.P. took an hour to tell me the same thing."

"I haven't got the time."

"You never did," she said.

"So I wasn't much for words."

"Just fighting," she smiled languidly. "Was it for a good cause?"

"I thought so at the time."

"And now?" she asked purposely.

"Time marches on. We all change."

Her eyes flashed with that look again and there was a sadness there. "It's too bad. Maybe some things can't be helped."

"Maybe they can."

"Oh?"

I watched her a good ten seconds, then asked, "Ever know a redhead named Mildred Swiss?"

"I read the papers."

"I didn't ask you that."

"Regan . . ."

"Just say yes or no."

"Can it be that simple?"

I knew what she was getting at. I pulled out my wallet, let it dangle open so she could see the pinholes in it and the impression that my badge had made against the leather after so many years of being compressed there. I said, "Let me put it this way. I know about the agency and I know about the sideline. If I wanted to I could probably break the thing, but there's never been a demand for it so I'm not pushing. If we got on you there would be so much hell to pay with the pressure that would come on from the power circles it wouldn't be worth the effort. I'm not here officially and frankly, I don't give a damn what you do with your time and energy. It's a sophisticated world these days, they tell me. Nobody gets the scarlet letter pinned on any more and what used to be condemned is currently condoned. Maybe it will get better and maybe it will get worse. It isn't my job to buck the trend. I just do what I'm told to do and do it damn well. At the moment I'm trying to do something on my own. I asked you a question. It doesn't go down in the files and I'm not saving up information until later."

"You *are* a wordy bastard after all, Regan." Her mouth opened and she laughed at me pleasantly. "All right, yes. I knew her. She didn't work for me."

"True, kid?"

"True, Regan."

"How did you know of her?"

Madaline shrugged and pushed back a wave of raven hair from her face. "Things come to me. One has to know the competition even if they're small operators. I can make out quite a list like her from memory."

"Whore?"

"Not the usual variety. She was on call with the Mays setup until the District Attorney broke it, then she was seen around working independently." She frowned, then added, "Not really working at it . . . more like she was looking for something solid."

"Marriage?"

Madaline nodded noncommittally. "Inwardly, they're all like that, I think."

"What about you?" I prodded, grinning.

Her eyes held steadily on mine. "I thought about it once. It would never have worked. I've seen too much of the raw thing." The black deep was there again before she looked away.

"Anything work for the Swiss girl?"

"Not that I know of. She settled into an apartment and was kept on the side by Ray Hilquist."

"The bookie?"

Madaline bobbed her head. "Confidante of millionaires. Probably the biggest in the area until he died in that accident."

I didn't bother telling her that it wasn't an accident. It looked that way because it was planned that way and no evidence could prove differently, but to a pro the thing smelled of murder and the books were still open on it. High finance bookie operations were syndicate business and somewhere along the line Ray Hilquist had soured out.

"What was she doing before she died?" I asked her quietly.

Again, that little shrug. Madaline said, "I didn't follow her career. She probably passed on into other hands." She turned her head and looked at me, a funny expression on her face. "I can ask around," she said. "Shall I?"

I got up and put on my hat, unconsciously hitching up the service revolver that wasn't there any more. "I'd appreciate it," I said. I walked to the door, stopped and turned around. "Lunch sometime?"

Madaline grinned at me like she did the time I took the guys off her back. "I'd appreciate it," she repeated in my own solemn tones.

*   *   *

On Saturday George Lucas met me outside the building where they had the departmental hearing with that same crooked grin and handed me the large manila envelope holding the five thousand dollars somebody had made me a present of for the favor of committing murder. "We had it made, buddy."

"The commissioners didn't think so."

"Okay, so you're on suspension until the details of the missing Marcus files are cleared up. At least they're only attributing it to negligence. The most you can get is a reduction in grade and a beat in the wilderness."

"Five grand isn't worth it."

"You forgot my ten percent."

"So deduct it." I held the package out.

He didn't touch it. "I already did," he laughed. "Now can we get down to business? How about some chowder at Vinnie's?"

A cab took us there and Vinnie gave us a table at the back of the room. We were the only ones in the place. I was wondering if Jerry Nolan would show up, but it was still a little early for him.

George held out his package of butts and I shook my head. He lit one up for himself and sucked in a haze of smoke. "How was the plant made in your apartment, Pat?"

"No trouble. Commercial type lock. Whoever got in used a key."

"Who has access to yours?"

I grunted at him and rubbed the stubble on my jaw. "I went all over that. Two possibilities. Somebody had a regular passkey that bonded locksmiths use or an impression was made from my own. It's on the same ring as my car keys and when I park it and use a department car I forget the damn things sometimes."

George's eyes half shut. "Argenio?"

"Why not?"

"You think he'd go that far?"

I shrugged, thinking about the way he hated my guts. "He wouldn't be the first one."

"That puts him on the take."

All I did was look at him.

"Nobody's ever laid anything on him," he said.

"Argenio smells bad," I told him.

"Say it slowly."

"He enjoys the rough stuff. I've seen him deliberately . . . oh, hell."

"Go on."

"It's nothing I can explain." I stared across the table at him. "Remember Welch, the cop on the south side we called the Dutchman?"

"How can I forget him."

"So he killed six or seven guys. Line of duty stuff, but he enjoyed it. Later he went too far with his pleasures and wound up doing time. Argenio's like that."

"You can't prosecute on suspicions, friend."

"Maybe I'll frame him," I said.

"I wouldn't put it past you."

I grinned at his tight expression and said, "Maybe I won't have to. My nose tells me he's not a square cop. One day he'll fall. Just don't sweat me, Georgie. I won't louse it up. Now let's get with the business."

I took an hour to give him the details of what I had lined up on Marcus' operation and the probable way they could set it up again. I had lived with it so long I was thinking like them and could almost see the rearrangement. George let me finish, taking it all down and stored his notes in his pocket.

"Okay," he said, "I'll get on it. Your loot ought to buy enough help to make it easier. Call me every once in a while."

"Don't worry." He laid a bill on the table to cover the check and walked out.

When he was gone I dialed Jerry Nolan at his office, and when he was on I said, "Regan, Jerry."

"I heard the results of the trial."

"Not over yet. They'll have to kick the negligence bit out. What I did was S.O.P. and you know it."

"I hope the commission does. What's up?"

"Get me copies of the body shots of Marcus. I'm at Vinnie's."

"Hell, man, you saw them," he said.

"So I want to do it again. I'm thinking straighter now."

Jerry let out a resigned breath over the phone. "Okay, stay there. Give me a half hour."

Twenty minutes later he was sitting where George had been and I had the eight-by-ten glossies spread out in front of me. They weren't very pretty. Four different angles were covered, the details clear in every one. All six shots had taken Leo Marcus in his face, the first one blowing off the pinkey of his left hand as he tried to protect himself from his killer in that last second. Blood, brain, bone and hair were splattered against the fieldstone of the fireplace and the rest of him was lying in the remains of the fire that had cooked the top part of his torso to charred remains.

"Nice job," I commented drily.

Jerry looked at me, his face tight. "We would have bought the mistaken identity bit if it weren't for the finger. It was stuck under the mantle. Two teeth from his plate were smashed into the log and three others with part of the plastic work intact were on the floor. In this case it was a special job and identifiable. The oral surgeon who did the work gave us an absolute position and our lab confirmed it."

"Yeah, I know," I said. "Nothing else he could be identified by?"

"Hell, who needed it? No . . . nothing. No surgery, no broken bones, but if you don't think we didn't go all the way, get this. We brought in two of his broads. They took a damn close look at his privates and confirmed. You like that bit?"

"No."

Jerry gave an exasperated snort. "Why not?"

"When they saw him before he was in a highly emotional state."

"Oh, balls."

"That's what I mean."

I sat there looking at the mess that had been Leo Marcus, the mess that I had made. There was no remorse, just the antagonizing feeling that I hadn't been alive enough to know what I had done because if it had been me I would have wanted to see every damn slug splash into his fat face, the same goddamn face that had broken others with a single look and had winked more into sudden death because they had displeased him. That one face had hooked kids into the big H, steered the unknowing into the bright eyed things that knew all the answers and died early by their own hands, squeezed too many into shapeless forms whose minds were his . . . people, but not by the standards I knew.

"Jerry . . ."

"What?"

"I wish it *had* been me."

"You sure it wasn't?"

"No."

"Why?"

"It wouldn't have happened so fast. I would have destroyed him slowly then let the law take care of him in that terrible, tantalizing way it has until he sat there crowded up against the arms of the big chair in Sing with the hood over his head and the electrodes on with all the witnesses watching and hoped he could hear them puke when the top of his head started to smoke from the juice going through him. No, it wasn't me."

"I know," Jerry said. "Now I know."

"You do? Why?"

"Because you aren't capable of simple murder. I've seen you smoke out killers before. You lived with this one too damn long, Regan."

"I'm still living with it."

"Then give me the answers."

I shuffled the photos like cards and stacked them and handed them back to him. "Somebody's on top of Marcus. His time was up. They wanted him out and they got him out. I was the sucker to take the heat off them. It didn't work."

"Who, Regan?" Jerry asked me. His face was a blank mask, a professional mask no different from the one the punks saw in the interrogation rooms.

"Find out. That's your business. I don't carry a badge any more."

"Or a gun?"

"I might do that. The hoods don't mind. The punks take pleasure in it. The proper civilians terrified by the stupid Sullivan Act and forgetting they have the protection of the Constitution unrestricted by jerks are too obsessed by legal interpretations to pack one when they should may be like that. But not me, Jerry. I'm not a proper civilian any more."

"You haven't been kicked off the force."

"You're damn right."

"Stay cool, buddy."

"Like hell. You know better. We can't exist cool, can we? Somebody has to move. It's my neck on the block."

"So you processed it. If anybody was in a position to know who was on top of Marcus, it's Patrick Regan . . . you. Something had to show. He was hand picked by the rest of the Syndicate . . . he worked his way up, proved his worth every damn inch of the way and was a power. You don't blast power out that easily. They have their own machine inside the big one and *coups d'état* aren't easy."

"For someone it was," I reminded him.

"You're crazy," he said.

"That's what the D.A.'s lad tried as a last resort when the trial was on."

"Shit."

"What else is new?"

To keep calm, Jerry grabbed at his butts, lit up a smoke and deliberately sat back looking at the ceiling. "Give me one idea," he finally mused.

"Did Van Reeves contact you about the Swiss broad?"

"Uh-huh."

"She was the redhead, buddy."

His eyes came down from the ceiling and searched my face. *"Now* you tell me."

"Last contact was Ray Hilquist. She lived with him."

"You son of a bitch. Where do you pick it up?"

"I'm fighting for my life," I said. "Remember?"

Jerry took another pull on the cigarette, his features thoughtful now. "Hilquist and Leo Marcus used to be tied in together. Just little things. Nothing worth pulling them for, but they were close." He wasn't looking at me now. He was reviewing the records mentally, pulling out the files in his mind the way cops do, remembering the little things that count. "They had a split once," he told me. "A broad was involved. Word got out that the wheels in the Syndicate called a meeting and pulled them back together, otherwise it was an 'or else' deal. They didn't like some twist interfering with business. No sweat after that. Too much action was involved. You have posed an interesting thought, Regan."

"Keep on it."

"I will." He leveled his eyes at me. "But you stay cool," he said as he got up. "When you're thinking you scare me."

"I'll scare a lot of people before it's through," I told him.

CHAPTER FOUR

STAN THE PENCIL wasn't hard to find. Like all the rest, he had his money rounds; the habituals with the two bucks, the fivers, the ten spots who waited for him in the right places to pick up their cash and slap it on the nose of some nag running the circuit. To him it was a living, two fifty a week with a few weeks in the workhouse when the administration needed a patsy to pad the news reports.

All expenses paid and his wife and kids supported while he was staring at the bars wondering when the legislature would legalize off-track betting like the people wanted despite the pious claims of the backwards-collar gooks and the political slobs who went their way.

I found him at The Shamrock making his book in a cheap pad, his eyes too suddenly round at what he saw in my face. I said, "Talk, Stan. Let's take a table somewhere."

"Look . . ."

"I'm off the force, Stan, but I can still break you in little pieces. Here and now. Your choice."

"So all right. Talk. It's cheap."

114

I grabbed his arm, pushed him to a table and called for a couple of beers. When the waiter brought the steins I sipped the top off mine and put it down and watched the wet circles it made on the table top. "You were there that night, Stan."

"Was I called as a witness?"

"Nope."

I let my eyes drift up to his, feeling the air go through my teeth again. "You've been around, boy. You know the ropes and the angles. Nothing gets past your kind. I thought nothing did through me, but something did. What was it?"

"Look, Mr. Regan . . ."

"Think, buddy. It's your arm. Left or right first?"

Stan The Pencil was scared. His throat bobbed convulsively and a vein in his temple throbbed too damn hard. "Mr. Regan . . . it was like they said. You got looped. Hell, I'd do what I could if . . ."

"There was something. I came in that bar sober."

"You had a headache. You was eating aspirins."

"I'd just bought them, Stan. An unopened box at the drugstore on the corner. I had six. It's an occupational hazard."

"So I didn't see nothing. No kidding, Mr. Regan . . ."

"Who slipped me a dose?"

He could hardly keep his hands folded in front of him. "Honest, Mr. Regan, it was like you had too much. So who was there? Them crazy artists, Popeye Lewis and Edna Rells, they ain't done nothing. Who could louse you up? You know old Popeye. He got nothing going for him except his paintings and fifty million bucks he hates. That nutty Edna he lives with is just as bad. All that loot and they shack up in a garret even if he does own the whole joint. He won't live off nothing his old man left him, just what they make with that crazy smear they sell. Me, so what did I do? Make a few contacts? I thought it was a good party."

"Where did the redhead come in?"

"Who knows?" he said. "Dames were all over the place."

"You saw her?"

"I saw plenty of broads. She latched on when you started the big pitch. Come on, Mr. Regan."

"How long have I known you, Stan?"

"Like maybe five years."

"Ever get yanked?"

"Hell, you weren't on that detail."

"Phones were all over the place," I reminded him. "I could have assigned it anytime."

"All right, all right. You were square. What you want from me, anyway?"

"The redhead."

Stan The Pencil's hands were in tight knots, the fingers twisted together. "Like she drifted over. You pitched, she caught. I cut out about then. I don't know from nothing. I told them all that."

"You know her?" I watched him closely.

He caught the funny look in my eyes and said, "I know her now. Not before. I seen it in the papers."

"Let's think back."

"What for?"

"Leo Marcus and Hilquist."

"Mr. Regan . . ."

"Stop bullshitting me."

His face got sullen and his eyes dropped to his hands.

I said, "What's the racket talk?"

"Some broad," Stan said softly. "This gonna hurt me?"

"No."

"Marcus fixed it. What difference does it make now?"

"Because I got fixed too," I said.

Very simply he looked up and said, "I'm more scared of them than you, Mr. Regan. What now?"

"Nothing, buddy," I said. "You can blow now."

He hadn't told me anything, but he'd think he had and he'd be different later.

I got out and walked. My apartment was fifteen blocks away but I had to think about it. A month gone sitting on a bail bond because they wanted to get it over with in a hurry, the eyes of a guy who had been close friends looking at you speculatively, the hatred of the press and the animosity of the public because they thought a hard-working career cop took five grand instead of his life's work. Nuts.

The rain started in a gentle mist at first, working up to a great gout that caught me on the corner of Eighth Avenue and Forty-ninth and when I walked through it, ignoring all its malicious fury, developed a rumble with heat lightning in the west that growled its displeasure at me.

I said, "Drop dead," toward the sky and kept walking while people watched curiously. Screw them too, I thought. If they knew who I was, they'd spit. The killer cop. He had gotten away with murder.

Well, thank somebody for twelve good men and true who had bought the story.

I hoped they were right.

There was still a chance they weren't.

* * *

I went over it again, knowing the odds I was up against. I reached the apartment and studied the old brownstone from

116

the outside, realizing that anybody could get inside there. Hell, for a pro, you could get anywhere. A key was easy to get. I inserted my own in the lock, turned it and pushed the door open. It was only a three room flat you could expect a bachelor cop to occupy, nothing special no matter how hard you looked. The only extravagance was the wall safe with nothing in it outside a will, a birth certificate and two diplomas, compliments of the butcher downstairs who thought I needed more security. The Marcus file had been stowed in the false bottom of the rectangular bottom of the waste basket by the old desk I used, a nothing place an ordinary housebreaker would have missed and a pro looking for the right thing in the right place found. The five grand was in a new place, too damn obvious, an area above the unpainted pine that formed a ceiling in the bedroom closet.

It was newly cut and that was what had made it all the more damning.

Out of curiosity I checked the apartment. The signs of white dust from the print teams the department sent in were still showing on the furniture, wisps here and there like an untidy woman would make from powdering after a bath, the *stigmata* of the professionals taking care of their own. *Or frying him if they had to.*

I lay down on the bed, listening to the air going out of the mattress with a soft hiss and closed my eyes, thinking of how nice it was to sleep and be away from it all. There was a sweet smell of pleasure there, a sensual odor of the far-off things that could never be attained for someone like me and sleep was the utmost pinnacle of desire. It was a gentle, wafting breeze that talked to me from way down deep and out of the downy fluffiness of it all I could hear a strange voice that had turned us into the wild assed bastards they couldn't beat with all of the Nazi deviousness and the man kept saying, "They'll try anything. If it's foreign to you, cut out and run. Shoot. No matter who. Blow out your breath and get away. They have chemical warfare to offset our superiority in noxious gases. They want you. Remember . . . *YOU. You* have information. They'll do anything. They'll do . . ."

My eyes opened on his words as if I were years back in a different place and I remembered the rules. I cut and ran, hit the door, opened it and lay face down in the empty doorway gasping for breath while my senses came back to me.

I was lucky. It had all seemed so nice. Like freezing to death in the snow when you thought you were nice and warm all the time. I found the unlabeled can under the mattress that had been activated by my weight. A simple thing that could have been a shaving cream container or a deodorant spray if

117

it hadn't been a deadly sleep inducer from which I never would have awakened.

After the windows were opened and the odor gone, I stuck the can in the refrigerator, locked up and dropped into the sleep I should have had in the beginning.

Somebody really wanted me dead in the worst way.

* * *

Even when you're a cop with a cloud over you, certain avenues are open. I took the canister up to the lab, where Sergeant Ted Marker looked at it before turning it over to the other specialists, letting me sit in the big chair by his desk while we waited for the analysis report.

For me, they did it fast. Ted's assistant came back in an hour with the can and an elaborate report. Ted studied it a moment before laying it on his desk, then read it over again to be sure. "German compound," he finally said. "We called it FS-7, Roderick Formula."

"What's that mean?"

He peeled off his glasses and looked at me. "Nerve gas. Unassuming and deadly. The trap was cute. You're supposed to be dead. What's inside you, Regan?"

"I'm motivated."

"Stop the crap."

Ted let a smile flicker across his usually glum face. "It was set up very easily. Like all aerosol bombs, small pressure sets it off. It was put under the springs of your bed. You pushed the button yourself."

"I'm glad I didn't have company."

"The value of being a lonely bachelor," he smiled.

"Knock it off." I leaned forward in the chair. "It isn't a domestic compound?"

"I haven't seen it since '45. One of the end products of the Nuremberg trials. It was exposed there."

"Like Sentol?"

"You think a lot, Regan."

"I'm supposed to," I threw at him. "What about the container?"

"German surplus. Somebody has access to unauthorized supplies. Outside of what was released to our own agencies, this stuff was all supposed to be destroyed."

"Somebody had a sense of the future," I grimaced.

His answer was quick. "Why?"

"To take care of people like me."

He nodded, looked at the report a moment, then came

118

back to me. "Some have a great sense of timing. They think ahead. They can wait."

"How could they get this stuff?"

Ted made a gesture with his shoulders. "How do the punks get guns?"

"That easy?"

"That easy. Money can buy almost anything."

I got up and put my hat on, thinking of the five grand somebody had left in my room. "Almost," I said.

Al Argenio came in as I said it, a small box in his hand. He hadn't shaved that morning and his face had a hard, swarthy look, a guy who had been up all night. He was all badge, gun and efficiency, and he gave me a hard leer and said, "What are you doing here, bum?"

He thought I was going to walk past him and ignore the remark. It was the second mistake he made with me. I laid one on those black chops of his that slammed him into the wall with a glassy stare in his eyes, awake enough to hear what I said but not awake enough to do anything about it. "Watch your tongue, slob," I said.

The others looked at me, hid their grins and didn't stop me from going out. None of them liked him either.

Downstairs, I used the pay phone to call the Murray Hill number. The one in the book got me to the PBX board, but the old badge number and the tone of voice got me Miss Mad on a private phone, that cool voice with the throaty timbre saying hello with that little tinge of anticipation I had hoped to hear and I said, "Regan, sugar. We alone?"

"I hope so."

"Lunch?"

"I hope so."

"You won't get shook? A cop isn't exactly a company president."

"In your circles I wouldn't be considered great company for a date unless it was in the line of duty, would I?"

"My circles aren't the old ones right now, honey . . . so it's a date. The Blue Ribbon on Forty-fourth?"

"You never change, do you?"

"Why should I, baby?" I asked her. "About two-thirty . . . the crowd will be gone."

* * *

The crowd was gone, but the regulars were there, saw her come in and join me and grinned in appreciation. She went through the bar, crossed into the booth behind Angie and sat down in the chair he held out for her.

119

"How many years has it been, Patrick?"

"Maybe twenty-five."

"The first time you ever asked me out to lunch before."

"Would you have accepted before?"

Something had happened to her eyes. The bottomless well wasn't there any more. "You'll never know," she said. "Shall we wait to eat or talk now? I know it isn't a cruise for you."

"Let's keep it like between old friends. You're easy on the eyes and it makes talking a pleasure."

"Okay, old friend. Just don't ask me one question."

I anticipated what she had in her mind and said, "Like what made you get into the racket in the first place?"

Madaline nodded sagely. "I might decide to tell the truth for a change. I never have before. The others all expected nice scandalous statements tinged with sensuality they could savor with all the gusto of a gourmet and I fed them what they wanted to hear. The truth is very simple and quite sordid."

"Then save it until you're ready."

She watched me, her fingers toying with the napkin. "You're probably the only one who would understand it."

The waiter took our orders then, brought a pair of drinks to sip at while we waited for the duckling he had suggested and I lifted the glass in a silent toast. "To now, Mad."

She winked, sampled the drink and put it down slowly. "I have news for you, Regan."

I waited.

"Let's call it hearsay. No confirmation. For your information I put the question to some of the kids and it didn't take them long to come up with some oddball facts."

"Like what?"

"Ray Hilquist may have set up Mildred Swiss, but she wasn't completely cooperative. She had been seen around with Leo Marcus in out-of-the-way places while she was supposed to be keeping Hilquist's bed warm."

"What the hell did Leo have to pull in a broad like her?"

Madaline pursed her mouth and shrugged. "Who can tell about women, Regan? Maybe they like most what they can't have."

"You know the Syndicate stepped in and cleaned up the deal?"

She nodded gently and picked up her drink. "That's the strange part."

"What is?"

"Leo was much bigger than Hilquist. It should have gone in his favor if there was a squabble." She drank, put the glass down and asked me, "Ever consider that?"

"I gave it a thought. Maybe they didn't figure little Millie

Swiss was right for their top man. Okay for Hilquist, but something Marcus wouldn't miss after a while."

"Possibly. They use computers in the rackets these days." Then she shook her head again, her face thoughtful. "I don't buy it. I've seen too damn much. I know those people."

"Oh?"

She said, "It was in the last couple of weeks before you shot . . . before Marcus was killed he was seen with Mildred Swiss. The kids told me it looked like love . . . all quiet and cozy, stars in her eyes, hand holding under the table and that sort of garbage. She was still in the apartment Hilquist had . . . the lease was paid in advance and he had left her enough spending money to keep her going for a year anyway after he died." Madaline grinned at me. "She was a lucky little twist. Most of them don't make out that well."

"A cozy situation," I said. "If Marcus did go for the broad he could have arranged Hilquist's accident, then took his time about moving in so no finger gets pointed at him."

"You're forgetting one thing," she said.

"What?"

"The wheels in the Syndicate don't like intramural rivalries. They'd go after anybody acting independently of their instructions, especially if it would jeopardize their operations."

"That only leaves two conclusions then," I said. "Either it *was* an accident or they arranged for it to happen."

"What do you think, Regan?"

"I don't know. It'll all too damn pat."

Before we could get into it deeper the waiter brought the lunch in and set down the plates. At the same time a foursome drifted by, picked the table next to us and sat down, so we relaxed into casual conversation, finished and went back out to Forty-fourth Street, where we waited for a cab.

I flagged one down and helped her into it, keeping my eyes off the flash of white that showed above the nylon hose momentarily, and she grinned when she spotted my prudishness. I said, "Check it out further if you can. I'll be at the apartment this evening and you can reach me there."

Madaline made a kiss of her lips and nodded. "Sure. I like to pay off my obligations."

"Go . . ."

"Uh-uh . . . none of that talk," she laughed.

* * *

Popeye Lewis and Edna Rells had been playing at the common-law marriage game for a long time. In the beginning

121

they had been part of the freedom loving sect who had a distaste for permanent ties and decided to try it on for size until it was over, but after four years it still wasn't ended and they had taken on all the semblance of old married couples without the benefit of law.

The building Popeye had bought with the millions he inherited was the only dip into the estate his father had left him. The renovations came out of his earnings as an oil painter and it was hurting him to be successful. He and Edna would rather have lived as true peasants. Between the two of them they had a five-figure annual income, a crazy sex life and were the envy of the phonies who ran down their talents at the same time they cultivated them for their whiskey handouts and fabulous parties.

Popeye waved me in, a brush between his teeth and his beard clotted with paint. Edna was studying a half-finished canvas, standing beside a full length mirror with a smock thrown over her hastily. I knew she had nothing on under it. The picture was a profile nude of herself and she was her own model. She was irritated at the interruption, stamped her foot with impatience and grinned, "Why the hell should I be bashful on your account, Regan? You know what a naked woman looks like?"

I glanced at the picture. "Now I do."

"Then go talk to Popeye," she told me. With a hitch of her shoulders she tossed the smock off and went back to studying herself in the mirror and putting the impression down on the canvas. She was quite a woman. Quite. But somehow there was no indecency to it at all. It was like looking at a bowl of fruit. Not really . . . but something like that.

Popeye ignored it all and popped open a can of beer and held it out to me. "I was going to send a card of congratulations, Regan. I didn't know if you'd appreciate the joke."

"Wouldn't have mattered."

He pushed over a bar stool and wiped it off. "Sit down. What's the word?"

"The redhead."

"Ah, yes, the redhead."

"It didn't come out at the trial."

"One of many that night, my boy. What about her?"

"She's dead."

"So I heard. Spud mentioned it in passing this morning."

"You saw the papers?"

"I did and she was there." He drank half the can off without a stop, took a deep breath and went on. "You were riding high, that night, buddy-o. I played it down on the stand . . . just answered the questions, but if I didn't know you better

122

I'd say you were mainlining for the first time. I never saw you like that before. What the hell happened?"

"You think I killed Leo Marcus?"

"Regan, I couldn't care less . . . but no. You talked it up a lot, but you're too square for that kind of action. Where'd you really get the load?"

"Somebody goosed me with a mickey."

"Who? That kind of stuff doesn't go at the *Climax*. Not with a cop, even for a joke."

"It wasn't a joke."

Popeye dumped the rest of the beer down, opened another can and offered me one. When I shook my head he said, "Why were you there, friend? That wasn't your beat any more."

"Al Argenio used to go with a hatcheck girl from the place."

"Ah, Helen the Melons. Quite a spoonful. Size forty-four chest. They weren't *simpatico,* kiddily. He used his badge to bump the opposition out of the way and that old Helen the Melons didn't like. She craved attention and appreciation of her superabundant mammaries. That was her come on, her stock in trade, her excuse of the un-necessity of education and her hope for the future. She did great with casual trade, but to get close to her you'd have to stand behind her or be crowded out of the way. Now you give me Edna there, who is only a simple thirty-eight . . ."

"Go up a stick," Edna said without taking her eyes off the mirror.

"True artist type," Popeye smiled.

"What happened to the melons?"

Popeye nursed his beer again and grunted. "Too much Al Argenio. She asked for a transfer. Nobody told poor Al . . . he wasn't the popular type . . . but she's over in Brooklyn at the Lazy Daisy inhaling at the natives."

"What's this transfer bit?"

He put the can down and picked up a cigarette. His eyes were suddenly sober. "You know the *Climax?*"

"How?"

"Check the ownership. Like it's a Lesbian joint mostly and the squares come in for a look and pay the freight. It cracks a big nut. One of the many holdings in the hands of that abstraction you people call the Syndicate."

"Who passed that on?"

"My lawyer who's beating his balls off to get me straightened out. He has me followed, tries to prove I lead a life not conducive to a solid citizen who owns most of three corporations and can draw on a fat bank account. He just don't know, man. He shows me where I hang out in a den of iniquity run by a nest of thieves. He wants me back in grey flannel suits attending board meetings."

"I thought Stucker owned the *Climax*."

"You aren't hep, old boy. Maybe it looks like he does, but he pays off to some funny people then. I've been around there a long time and it was Leo Marcus' boys who made those weekly visits. But just don't try to buck the system. It's liable to explode on you. They have accountants and machines and front men all making up to a tidy little sub rosa government that pulls a lot of weight. You see what it cost you for prying."

"You seem to know a lot, Popeye."

"I got big ears, a lot of talkative friends and a sharp insight into this wild world of money-hungry denizens. Why do you think I pulled out of it?"

"Everybody to their own taste." I looked at him, flipping the empty can into a trash basket. "You never finished with the redhead."

"So she was there. So were a lot of others. You were quite a card."

Edna Rells stepped out from behind the canvas, a lovely naked figure with a paint streak just above her navel and a brush tucked in her hair. "With all the crowding, Spud couldn't get to the table. She took the tray and served the drinks. One belt later and you were all over her."

"Thanks, sugar."

It had been as easy as that. She was planted there or had followed me there. She picked the right time and loaded me. I picked up my hat and pushed myself off the bar stool. "See you around," I said. "I appreciate the talk."

"What talk? You came here to discuss art," Popeye said solemnly.

I looked at Edna who twisted her hips and threw a bump at me with a leer. Only the brush came out of her hair and left a smear across one ample nipple when it fell. "Yeah, art. I'm all for it. You guys are nuts."

* * *

The redhead, Leo Marcus and me. Somebody had missed the boat in planning the State's case. They should have tied in the redhead and I would have been on the death list at Sing Sing. The D.A. could have made it look like we were in it together to knock off Marcus, that in my hatred I had somehow recruited her. Now she was out of it altogether and if they wanted to build a new case they could try it on me for

124

size. Sooner or later the D.A.'s boys would be asking questions, they'd have some answers to Mildred Swiss' past and they'd be asking me where I was when she was dumped.

So . . . where was I? My contacts had been limited. I had been walking and thinking. I was ready to be a patsy again. I needed an alibi, but before I could nail it down I had to find out when she had died.

I waited until I saw Ted Marker come out of the building and followed him from across the street and half a block back to the subway station, made sure none of the others were around and caught up with him as he was buying tokens from the attendant on the platform. He could have used his badge to go through the gate for free but never bothered to. I came up beside him, got two tokens and said, "Wait for me, Ted."

He nodded curiously, went through the turnstile and stood behind the crowd of commuters. We went three stops and upstairs to a bar and grill where everybody was watching the last inning of a ball game and ordered a pair of beers at the counter.

"What's it about, Pat?"

"How'd the make go through on Mildred Swiss?"

"Checked right out."

"They establish the time of death?"

"On the nose. The Medical Examiner's autopsy report checked with a watch in her pocket that had stopped. Five-fifteen."

"Why was the watch in her pocket?"

"Because the clasp had been broken."

"It was daylight then," I said. "They don't usually go in during the day. Not female suicides. They think about their hair and their clothes and the water isn't a good prospect for death. It's filthy with garbage and sewerage and stinks."

"That's suicide. She was murdered."

I looked at him.

"Fingernails broken from where she clawed somebody apparently. Her hands had been well manicured. She had a bruise on her head that could have knocked her out. There was a hairdressing appointment on a card in her wallet for the next day. She made the date by phone and didn't seem disturbed at all."

"It figures. One odd thing."

"What's that?" Ted asked.

"Why didn't the body sink?"

"Simple. She was hung up on a piece of driftwood, a plank with one end waterlogged had nails that snagged her clothes. She wasn't in the water very long at all."

Mentally, I checked the time. I had been in the apartment all that while and nobody had seen me come in or spoken to me until I had gotten Spud's message. It didn't have to be planned that way, but it could put me back in the hot water again. The other alternative was that somebody wanted Mildred Swiss dead, just plain dead and quickly.

Ted finished his beer and said without taking his eyes from the TV: "Where do you fit in, Regan?"

"I don't know yet."

"I'm feeling your line of thought."

"Not good, is it?"

"Uh-uh," he told me. Then: "I asked some questions about that sleep gas. It took a while, but a smart boy in Washington provided some answers. Right after the war a batch got into this country mixed in a surplus deal. They couldn't pin it down, but there was a shady aspect about it. About ninety percent was recovered from the Ross and Buttick Warehouse where it was stored by a company who imported it among other things. Bensilee Imports. Legitimate firm operating since 1919."

"Who broke it down?"

"The O.S.S. discovered the stuff missing, then Washington moved and working with our department located the stuff. It was taken out to sea and dumped. Lot of publicity on it when it happened. They were afraid some kids would get into the stuff thinking it was DDT or something. The citizenry sent in truckloads of stuff for inspection, but none of it was that FS-7 derivative of the Roderick Formula."

Another little piece, I thought. *Publicity alerted the public to the potential dangers of the stuff, but it could have aroused the curiosity of other parties to its potential for their own activities.*

I said, "Any deaths attributed to its use?"

Ted Marker turned his head and said, "I was wondering when you'd ask. The man in Washington said there were two prominent Syndicate defectors who died mysteriously from undetected causes. It's a possibility, but wasn't detected. In each case the M.E. wasn't familiar with FS-7. Only the prominence of the dead men kept it open."

"And if I had died it would have looked like a natural thing . . . nobody would have shaken the room down and probed under the bed for a can until the landlord or a new tenant did . . . or the guy who planted the stuff came back. It could have been easy . . . he could have posed as a reporter, a new tenant . . . anybody."

"Cute. Again I say you were lucky."

"Nope . . . just filled with natural instincts." I finished the

126

beer and waved to the bartender for another round. "They figure out where the redhead got it?"

"Roughly. The tide was incoming, the rate of drift and time of death put it in the dock area around the Forties . . . providing the plank that held her didn't get snagged along the way. In that case it would have happened farther up. Anyplace along there you find traffic, drifters . . . well, hell, you know the area. Even in daylight it could have been arranged."

"Yeah, sure," I agreed.

Ted looked at his watch and I knew he was anxious to get going. "One more thing. I read everything available on the Sentol product. One thing it doesn't induce . . . in fact, inhibits it . . . is a person under its influence passing out."

"I was out cold when they found me there."

"That's what I mean. Sentol keeps the user awake like the goof balls the truckers use, but acting in strange directions."

"Positive?"

He nodded, his face grim.

"In that case I did it all on my own . . . that what you're thinking?"

"What do *you* think, Regan?" he asked me.

"A factor has been missed somewhere. Thanks for the time. Let's go."

CHAPTER FIVE

I BOUGHT a barbecued chicken at the delicatessen and brought it up to the apartment for supper. I hadn't taken time to clean up the place and it was beginning to look like a Harlem hovel with dirty dishes and damp towels all over the place. There was a note in my box, hand delivered from George Lucas, that I opened when I got the chicken on the table that simply said, "Give me a call."

When I tried his office the number didn't answer, so I sat down to the chicken, giving him time to get home. The light on the electric coffee pot blinked red, a signal that it was finished, so I rinsed out a cup and poured it full, sitting with my feet propped up on the table and a dripping drumstick in my fist.

That was when the bell rang. Before I opened it I took the .45 automatic I had liberated after the war, checked the load

127

and held it ready. I had to hold the chicken leg in my teeth to unlock the door and swing it open.

Madaline took all of me in with one sweep of her eyes, started a laugh, then stifled it behind a grin. "All you need is a cutlass to look like Blackbeard," she said.

"His name was Teach. Captain Teach."

"Okay, brains. But you sure do take a big mouthful." I yanked the chicken down and closed the door behind her. She took one look around and shook her head in disgust. "So this is how a cop lives," she said. "Can't you afford any better?"

"I'm not on the take, Mad. It's okay when it's clean. Who needs more?"

"You do. Why didn't you ever get married?"

"I sort of forgot to. Now who would have me?"

She smiled again, pulled up a chair at the table and reached for the other half of the chicken, pulling it apart delicately. "How much money have you got in the bank?"

"About twenty-two hundred bucks."

"Your life savings," she stated. "Get a woman who needs it."

"Forget it, kid. When I get a woman it's because she needs me and I need her. I still like the old-fashioned relationship." I poured her some coffee too, then sat back down again. "I didn't expect company."

"You said to call."

"There's a phone."

"Quit being so damn proud. Nobody recognized me. Your reputation is still intact . . . and enhanced if anybody did see me come in. How often do you get a broad in diamonds and minks into this garret, anyway?"

"Not more than twice a week."

"Sure," she laughed. "The chicken's good." Through a mouthful she added, "I have news again."

I sipped at my coffee, watching her. Something had changed in her eyes.

"There's a Jane Doe who had known Mildred Swiss since she came here. Both came from Europe and wound up in the same business. She saw Mildred the day she died . . . about noon time. They chatted for ten minutes on the street, walked a few blocks together and during that time Mildred gave the impression that she was going away for a trip. She was planning on an extensive wardrobe and couldn't help rubbing it in a little."

"She say who with?"

"As I said, it was a hint . . . an impression the girl got. She was elated, talked amiably, but that was all."

128

"Who was the girl? If she was the last one to see her alive the police . . ."

"I said she was a Jane Doe, remember? This is off the record, Regan."

"What's the rest of it?"

She took another bite of chicken and threw the bone down on the wrapping paper. "You're a shrewd one, Patrick. The Jane Doe wanted to talk more, but Mildred didn't have time. She was getting ready for a date."

"With a killer."

"Quite possible."

I put my cup down and tilted back in the chair. "Sooner or later something happens to most of them," I said. "Doesn't it make you sick? You're in the racket up to your pretty neck."

A cloud seemed to pass over her face and she looked down at her hands. When she decided to look up she said, "Then let me give you the answer I never gave anybody else. Yes, I'm in it. I went into it with my eyes open because it was the only answer to feeding an old man who was an alcoholic, paying medical expenses for an invalid mother and supplying the needs of seven other kids in the family. It was a deliberate move and I knew the right person to set me up."

"You could have gotten out. You did change the nature of the business."

"There was one thing that didn't change. I saw what happened to too many girls. I saw where they went and how they ended up. By keeping my hand in I was able to direct more of them out of it in time. Oh, hell, Regan . . . I know what you're thinking. I was still involved, but I got to know the right people and had enough going for me so that I could kill any heat that landed on the kids who got to know too much. There are those who say prostitution is better controlled. Funny enough, I'm not one. I'd like it abolished, but as long as the damn public demands it, the authorities accept it and the bastards behind the scene control it, I'll stay in where I can do some good when the time comes. That's my story, buy it or not."

"I'll buy it, Mad," I told her. "It might not be my way, but I'll buy it."

She reached over and put her hand on mine. "Thanks, Patrick. I was hoping you would." Her hand was warm, the pressure gentle and it was like the time she had thanked me silently in school when I came in chopped up after the fight, when she had done the same thing when I was at my desk and nothing more. It had been enough for me then. "Now . . . will you do me a favor?"

"Sure . . . what?"

"Let me clean up this fleabag."

I grinned at her. "Be my guest."

Downstairs I picked up two six packs of beer and brought them up and was content to sit there and watch the incredible efficiency of a woman used to service and attention doing the dirty work I could hardly face up to myself. She seemed to enjoy it, too, humming snatches of songs from the war years, laughing at the little things I said, content to let me sit and think while she let the years of luxury wash off her so that she was a kid again.

When she turned around her face was flushed, shiny with beads of sweat and her eyes were bright with living. The place was clean, too. She brushed away a wisp of hair that had fallen across her face, looking more lovely and younger than I had ever seen her.

"Better?"

"Perfect, doll, perfect. Do I pay you day wages?"

"A shower will do. I feel like a mess."

"You look good to me."

She grinned. "You're just saying that because it's true. Put some more coffee on."

While I filled the percolator I heard the shower running. I had a crazy warm feeling I never had before, like being part of something nice, something I never knew I wanted before.

The pot stopped bubbling as the light blinked red and I was pouring two cups when she came out of the bathroom. Someplace she had dug out my big old beach towel and had it draped around her like a sarong, another wound around her head turban fashion. She smelled of soap, and warmth radiated from her. One lithe leg jutted from the slit where the towel was knotted at her hip, the flesh firm and silky smooth, still showing a summer tan, the graceful curves swelling from a full calf into a thigh that blossomed with muscular maturity. The top of the towel was reluctant to conceal her breasts, trying to hold fast while each breath made it slip from its position until she almost swelled out of it.

We stood like that for what seemed a long time, looking at each other, seeing all without ever breaking that single, intense stare. Years ago it had happened too. We were young then, unaware of what was happening, knowing something had changed without being able to name it.

The first step we took together, touched with mutual desire, then her mouth was a rich, ripe furnace that melted into mine with a low moan of something too long suppressed and she pressed against me, her body feeling for every inch of me. The thrust of her body burst the tie of the knot in the towel and it dropped unnoticed at our feet, then I had all the

130

womanly texture of her in my arms, under my hands, taking everything she was offering.

I picked her up, deliberately stopped at the threshold of the bedroom door where she smiled up at me with the dreamy eyes of a bride, then crossed to the bed and laid her down gently.

Outside the noise of traffic dimmed and a slow rain began to beat against the window. Thunder rumbled across the roof of the city and the soft yellow of heat lightning brightened the room momentarily every once in a while. It was only when the wind shifted and the rain slanted in the half open window and sprinkled across the bed did we notice it. Unconsciously, I looked at my watch. Three hours had gone by.

"Time, Regan?"

"Plenty of time, kitten."

"It's been a long time coming, hasn't it?"

"Years and years."

"Will it ever happen again?" There was an expectant catch in her voice, a hushed quality as though she said more than she had wanted to. The hesitant fear was there in her face, but she had to wait for my answer now that it was asked.

I said, "We're funny people, you and I. Maybe we found something."

"Can we be sure?"

I touched the wild swell of her breasts and felt her quiver beneath my fingers. "Are you asking me . . . or yourself? Something would have to change. I can't."

"No . . . you shouldn't. I'm sorry, Regan. I never should have said it. The words . . . just spilled out. I'm not something to be proud of."

"Why not?" My words were sharp, said from between teeth held too tightly together. "I've seen people die, kid. I've helped them fall. I've pulled the trigger. I've been there and back so who the hell am I to look back and pass judgment. It's now and later that counts. Not the before part."

Madaline came to me with the fierce possessiveness of a tiger, saying things I knew she had never said to anyone else before and heard them repeated back to her. Her nails bit into my skin with frenzied delight, her body engulfing me with new, supreme love.

The phone ringing wakened us with its insistence until I rolled out and picked it up. "Regan?"

"Yeah?" It was George Lucas' voice.

"Where the hell have you been. I left a note and . . ."

"I just got in." I lied to save making excuses.

"Well, buddy, I want to see you. Important."

"Now? It's two a.m."

"It's your money, Regan. I said it was important."

"Okay, name a spot."

George named a bar on Sixth Avenue, and I told him I'd be there in thirty minutes. Madaline murmured when I shook her and opened her eyes. "Get up, Mad. Something's come up. I don't want you here alone."

"Oh, Pat . . ."

"Somebody tried to kill me here the other night. Let's not make it easy for him if there's another try."

Her eyes came wide open and I told her about it. She didn't take more than a few minutes to get dressed. I shrugged into my coat, slipped the .45 into my belt and held the door open for her. She started to step out into the hallway when I realized the mistake I almost made and slammed her back with a sweep of my forearm. She hit the wall, fell as I jammed the door shut and dropped beside her.

No noise. Just two tiny holes showed in the panel at waist level and something chunked into the wall at the other side of the room. Madaline's mouth was open with surprise as I said, "Somebody turned the light out in the hall." Then she saw the holes in the door and nodded abruptly.

I reached up and flipped the switch off, blanketing the room in darkness. "Stay there," I said. I felt the knob, turned it and eased the door open. Whoever was out there saw the motion and there was another almost silent *plop,* but I caught the wink of a muffled muzzle blast and triggered off a single shot at the pinpoint of light. The tremendous roar of the .45 split the night apart and feet pounded the stairs below with the heavy tread of someone in headlong flight. The door downstairs opened and slammed shut, but I didn't follow, knowing it could be a cute trap. He could have eased back behind the stairwell and be there waiting. I went inside, got my flashlight, poked the beam through the banister to search out the area, and when I was certain it was empty, went down and turned on the hall light.

Madaline joined me at the door, still shaking with fright. "What happened?"

"Another try. This time with a silenced gun. One of us is a target."

"One of . . ."

So she wouldn't be any more frightened than she was I said, "Me, most likely. Nobody knew you were here. They tried for me before. They're running scared now."

"Pat . . ."

"Let's go, Mad. He won't stay around now." I waited for someone to show, listening for a siren in case one of the neighbors had heard the shot and called it in, but either the walls were too thick or nobody cared. I flagged down a cab, gave him the address of the bar and climbed in. Madaline squeezed my hand, forced a smile and didn't say anything. I could still feel her trembling.

* * *

George had a corner of the bar to himself and the frown he wore turned into a grin when he saw Madaline and he held out his hands to her. "I'll be damned. Like a class reunion. How the heck are you, Madaline?"

"Scared. Good to see you again, George."

He looked at me and I roughed him in on what had happened. When I finished his eyes were narrow and hard. "The pressure is on, Regan. It can hit from any direction now. You're too much of a threat. What the hell is it you know?"

"A lot of things. Not much of anything."

"Well, I have something. Your money brought in some talk." He glanced at Madaline.

"It's all right," I said. "She's part of it with us. All on the same side."

"Before he died, Leo Marcus set up the Syndicate's new system. You had the old setup torn apart and the Syndicate got on his back for it. They held him responsible and dropped it in his lap. He had to get clear. Some way, he heisted the proof you had which put him back in the catbird seat with the Syndicate. Now here's the kicker. The top dogs in the organization took a jolt when they had their lawyers check on the reorganization plans. Leo Marcus had taken their money and built himself a separate little world with it. Most likely he planned to get the dough back in the pot before the loss was discovered, but he didn't act fast enough. They found it out and put out a contract for his kill that was accepted by a pair of hoods from Chicago."

"When was this?"

"The closest I could figure it was three days before Marcus died. That gave them time to reach New York and pull the job."

I shook my head. "They don't work like that and you know it. They generally take a couple of weeks to lay out the kill."

"Unless . . ." George started to say.

"Unless what?"

"They played it scientifically. They're pros and they saw a way to move fast. They tried to take the heat off themselves and the mob by setting you up. Hell, you were on suspension and burning up to get to Marcus and they couldn't ask for a

133

better sucker. You were handy and they hung it on you in a hurry. The Syndicate would have liked it that way."

"There's a hole in the story."

"Where?"

"The big boys wanted their money back too."

It was George's turn to shake his head no. "Not in this case. They could afford to let it go. They'd get it back in other ways, but they wouldn't care about it that much. A guy with a million doesn't miss a dollar. It's the principle of the thing. They don't want to establish any precedents by letting somebody in the organization get off with company funds."

"Damn," I said.

"There may be a contract out on you too, Regan," George said quietly. "Where do we go from here?"

I tossed down the beer the bartender brought and said, "The love of money is the root of all evil."

"What?" George frowned.

Madaline gave me a quick glance.

"I'll call you at the office, George. Stand by in case there's trouble."

"The departmental trial is tomorrow."

"I'll be there," I told him. I threw a bill on the bar and took Madaline by the arm and steered her outside. George had just grunted and called for another drink.

From the outside phone booth at the corner of Broadway I called Jerry Nolan and told him to meet me down at the diner near the precinct house. He swore and grumbled, but said he'd be there in fifteen minutes. When he got out of his car he was wrinkled and half dressed, a leather jacket thrown over his pajama tops. "You're a bird, Regan. I don't know why the hell I'm doing this." He looked at Madaline, recognition in his eyes. "What's she doing here?"

"I asked her, Jerry." I reached for her hand and he saw it.

His shrug said a lot of things. "Sure. What's up?"

"Where's Argenio?"

"Home in bed if he's smart. He was on the Scipio thing all day."

"Things ought to be quiet inside. Nobody should ask you any questions. I want you to check the M.P. reports."

"Who's missing?" he asked me.

"That's what I want to find out." I explained it to him quickly and he scowled.

"You got any idea how long that will take?"

"Maybe you'll be lucky."

"Damn it, Regan, I could be at that two-three days. Supposing it isn't on the reports?"

"Then check the skid row bunch. They're all permanent fixtures and somebody should know."

"Suppose it isn't this city?"

"Get cooperation from the other departments. We've done it before."

He rubbed his hand over the stubble on his jaw. "You think it's possible?"

"Don't you?"

"Could be," he nodded. "So it'll cost me some sleep and plenty of hell at home. The wife's complaining about the hours now and I'm not even bucking for promotion." He nodded good night to us and walked inside.

Madaline looked at me and said, "Can I ask what that was all about?"

"Better you don't know, sugar. Not now, anyway."

"Flatfoot," she grimaced pleasantly.

I saw a cab cruising and waved to it, got inside and gave the driver my address. Madaline raised her eyebrows at me. "Short night."

I nudged her with my elbow. "It's polite to wait until you're asked."

When I paid off the driver I waited until he was out of sight, made sure we were clear and went into the vestibule. I was finished taking chances. The light was on, the way was cleared and I had the .45 in my hand. Madaline's feet followed mine to the landing and I held her to one side while I opened the door.

My apartment was empty.

I closed and locked the door while Madaline shucked out of her jacket, then got a knife and icepick from the kitchen, found the three holes where the slugs had imbedded themselves in the wall and worked for twenty minutes prying them out without doing too much damage.

Madaline looked at the squashed lead pellets in the palm of my hand and touched their flattened surfaces with a forefinger. Not much was left of them. "Will a comparison test prove anything?"

"Ballistics expert?"

"I read a lot."

"I'm not interested in the gun, Mad. They're easy to get. It's the silencer and certain new chemical tests that will add things up."

"All right, my inscrutable friend, play games, excite my curiosity. I have ways of getting even, you know."

I dropped the slugs on the table and held my arms out. She came to me easily, her mouth tilted up, and her eyes were brand new, brand new. "Don't ever do that," I said.

"No . . . I never will, Regan."

135

CHAPTER SIX

THE morning shrouded the city in a pall of mist that dripped down the windows and laid a slick on the streets. A fog smelling of factory refuse and polluted river water crept in from the west, touching everything with its clammy fingers.

It was a death day out there. You could see it and feel it and taste it. It was the old man with the scythe taking his seat in the coliseum to watch the bloody action he knew would be there.

People hurrying to work had their heads down against the damp, eyeing each other suspiciously, dodging the sharp points of umbrella ribs and snarling over their shoulders when they were almost impaled. The tires of the cars hissed against the pavement and the taxis moved impatiently searching for riders. It wasn't bad enough for anyone to fight for their services yet and the drivers jockeyed toward the corners hoping to catch one of the undecided by stopping in front of them.

I grabbed one and packed Madaline in it and told the driver her office address, telling her I'd call later. She didn't want to leave, but realized she couldn't stay and kissed me goodbye gently, her fingertips caressing my face as she did. "Is it for real, Regan? Am I fooling myself?"

"It's for real, baby."

"Then there will be some changes made, darling," she told me. "I'll see you later."

The next cab past stopped for me and I told him where to go in Brooklyn.

Nobody was at the Lazy Daisy club except a porter who was carrying out the cartons of empty bottles and accumulated night's trash to the garbage cans beside the building. At night the place would be a garishly lit hangout for the wild money and the slum crowd from across the bridge looking for excitement, but by early daylight it was a drab, peeling slop-chute with all the earmarks of a sucker trap for the tourist trade.

The porter made me with one look and tried to get out of the way, but I yanked him back and said, "Don't duck, pops. I don't want you and there's no squeal."

"So what'cha want? I ain't . . ."

136

"Helen the Melons. She works here. Where does she live?"

The old guy shrugged. It was none of his business and she wasn't important enough to clam up for. "She got a pad at Annie Schwartz's house. Two blocks over." He gave the street and told me to look for the sign, then went back to his work after almost spitting on my shoes. He didn't like cops either.

Annie Schwartz was a beer-bloated woman with too-yellow hair and bad teeth who took one casual glance at me and spat out, "Cop."

"Right, Annie."

"Don't try rousting me, mister. This place is clean."

"Enough to stand an inspection from the fire department? Or how about a review of . . ."

"What're you after?"

"Blonde named Helen who works at the Lazy Daisy."

"Upstairs. Number three."

I walked past her and up the creaking stairs, found the door with a metal 3 tacked to it and knocked. Nobody answered and I tried the knob. The door swung inward on a wall of heavy perfume hanging in the musty air and the gentle rumble of Helen's snore.

She was stretched out on a bed completely naked, the covers kicked to one side, her mouth open and slack. Her nickname described her well. If she had been larger topside she would have had to walk on all fours. I pulled the covers back over her and shook her awake, listening to her mouth obscenities.

Finally, her eyes focused on me, her mind worked up a tirade to throw at me, then she recognized me and tried to shrink down beneath the blankets. Her voice was almost a whisper. "Regan . . . what . . . I didn't . . ."

"Don't sweat it, Helen."

She got a little more nerve then. "What right have you got to . . . listen, you got a search warrant or something? You looking for . . ." Then she saw the expression on my face and whimpered.

"What's your deal with Al Argenio, Helen?" I asked her quietly.

"Al? What's it to you?"

"If I ask you again it'll be the hard way. No trouble making a nice soft twist like you speak up. You should know that."

Helen tried to swallow but her mouth was too dry. She shook her head trying to get the meaning of things and failed. "Nothin's with him and me. So he chases after me alla time. I got tired of it. Alla time breaking things up when I got somethin' goin' with somebody who's got some dough. A

137

dozen times I got a guy who's willin' to spend it on me and he steps in and busts it. Alla time promises from him and that's all. I got tired and told him to blow. Him and his promises. Thinks he's gonna make it big and gimme what I want. Like hell. He ain't gonna make nothin'. So whatta I get? Lousy stocks he gimme for a present. Thinks they're hot stuff and it's paper. If he'd blow it on the ponies he might make it, but them damn stocks. You wanna see what he gimme? Look in that top drawer."

I took her advice and pulled open her dresser. A bundle of blue certificates held together with a rubber band were in the corner. Oil, gold, uranium stocks issued by strange-sounding companies were in the packet, all paying for somebody's exploratory work and a paid vacation. Buddy Al had a vice, all right. There were thousands like him that kept the sharpshooters in Cadillacs and fancy apartments.

"He find you yet?" I asked over my shoulder while I jotted down the stock names.

"If you did, he will. Now I got more trouble. He wants me he better come up with somethin' real. Right now I got a guy . . ."

"Save it," I said.

As I went out she yelled, "You tell him . . ."

But I shut the door on her and went back downstairs. Annie Schwartz was waiting with her fat arms crossed over her heavy chest trying to force a scowl through the fat wrinkles that seamed her face. "Quick, wasn't it?" I said.

Once I got back to Manhattan I called Jerry Nolan at the precinct station and asked him how he was making out.

He sounded tired and irritable. "Nothing in the files here. I'm checking out the departments upstate and in Jersey but it's going to be a while before I get anything." He paused, took a breath and added, "How long can this thing wait?"

"It can't, Jerry. Stay on it. Argenio there?"

"He came and went."

"Alone?"

"Yeah, why?"

"Just curious. I'll call back later."

I held the receiver down, dropped in another dime and dialed the Police Academy building. The officer at the PBX board who took my call told me Argenio had left a few minutes ago. I said thanks and hung up without giving him any more information.

Then I stood there and grinned a little bit. The bits and pieces were falling into place very neatly.

Going past the guys who worked in the lab wasn't easy. Until the trial that afternoon was over I was still a suspended cop better to stay clear of, no matter how good my record had been. A few nodded hello and two stopped to talk a minute, but most discreetly ducked out of the way and left me alone.

Ted Marker was over by the window, picking the charred remains of clothes from a cardboard box that was labeled as having come from a burned vehicle. I said, "Hi, Ted."

He grinned and pushed the box away. "You got plenty of nerve, Pat."

"For this job I need it." I reached in my pocket and took the slugs out I had dug from my wall and held them out to him.

"Comparison job?"

"Nope. Chemical analysis of the powder and metal."

"Against what?"

"They were fired through a silencer. Unless it was cleaned thoroughly, which is unlikely, the same traces will be on the silencer."

"Maybe," he said. "Where's the gimmick?"

I told him and watched the funny expression come over his face. "You'd better be sure, Regan."

"What can I lose? You can get to it, can't you?"

"No trouble. It makes me feel squeaky, that's all." He looked at the slugs again, his mouth tight. "What can it prove?"

"A link in the chain."

I went to turn away when I saw his books on the shelf. One had a slip of white paper marking off a page and I caught the word SENTOL on it. Ted said, "All the available information is right there."

"And you don't think it was Sentol?"

He gave a slight shrug. "You never should have passed out. I told you that. Not unless you had a bellyful of aspirin."

I swung around. "What?"

"Aspirin has a nullifying effect on the stimulant effect of Sentol."

"Ted," I said. "I had six aspirins before I went into the *Climax* that night."

His eyes tightened up again. "You sure?"

"Hell, I can prove it. I bought them and took them right there in the drug store on the corner of the block. The clerk gave me a drink to wash them down."

"That could have done it, then. But where did anybody get that damned drug?"

I let out a small laugh. "I bet I can guess. Want to work it out with me?"

"Damn right."

"When they found the FS-7 at the Ross and Buttick ware-

139

house, see who was on the detail. The records of assignment are available. Then check and see if any Sentol was in that consignment."

Ted gave me a startled look and snapped his fingers. "Wait a minute, Regan. For that last part I don't have to look. I remember it because we tested it in the lab. I was on vacation, but I saw the reports my assistant made out. Damn, I had forgotten about that."

"Then get on the first part."

"Will do." He paused, cleared his throat and said, "The trial's today, isn't it?"

"This afternoon. Three o'clock."

"Check back afterwards."

"Either way it goes?"

"Either way."

* * *

I reached George Lucas' office just before noon and caught him at his desk going over his arguments in my behalf at the trial. He looked up, waved me to a chair and said, "We got a rough one here."

"Argenio going to appear?"

"He doesn't have to. His signed report is enough." He put his pencil down and stared at me. "Why?"

I told him what I thought and watched him absorb it with interest. When I was done he said, "You're taking long chances with guesswork."

"It fits."

"Wait till it's proven."

I threw the notes I had taken from Helen the Melons' room on his desk. "How can I get some fast advice on those stocks?"

"Try your other lawyers, Selkirk and Selkirk. They're in that business."

"Give them a call."

I listened while George put the call through and rattled off the list. There was a short wait while the elder Selkirk fed him back the information, then he hung up. "They said don't buy in. It's junk. Goes at a high price and brings back nothing. Like trying to pull an ace out of a deck with one try. Occasionally one comes through, but the odds are against it, sucker stuff."

"What was the stuff worth?"

"About twenty grand worth in that list. That all?"

"As much as I know about."

140

"The trap is tightening," he smiled mirthlessly. "You think there's more?"

"You can ask around. He might have a safety deposit box. If you want I know a guy who owes me a favor and wouldn't mind going through his place looking for it."

"Don't take the chance."

"Maybe we won't have to." I got up and reached for his phone. "Mind?"

"Help yourself."

I told his secretary to get me Jerry Nolan at the precinct station and perched on the desk while I waited for him to answer. He came on and said, "Nolan here."

"Regan. What's new?"

"Nothing. Now let me eat my lunch."

I said, "You remember the dentist that confirmed the false teeth he made for Marcus?"

"Dr. Leonard Shipp. Now can I go eat?"

"Sure. See you later."

I hung up and told George I'd be back in an hour to go over things with him. He wanted me to stick around, but there wasn't enough time left any more. Things were beginning to move and I had to keep them going. I found Dr. Shipp listed in the directory and grabbed a cab to his West Side address, made him leave a patient to come out and talk to me, smelling of whatever was going on in his sterile white-tiled room.

He was a tall, angular man with impatient eyes behind his bifocals, annoyed at the interruption and wanting to get it over with quickly. He was the type who took the word "Police" at face value and didn't bother to ask about a badge.

"You had Leo Marcus as a patient for some time, didn't you?"

"I thought that was all over."

"Other pertinent details have come up."

His head jerked in a curt nod. "Mr. Marcus was a patient for some years. I extracted all his teeth and made the plates for him. There was no doubt about it. They were specially made and quite expensive. In fact, I made two sets for him."

"Oh?"

"Very common procedure. A lost or broken set can be very embarrassing."

"No difference?"

"They were identical."

"Thanks, doctor."

I left him and went back outside. One thing I knew. I had seen all of Leo Marcus' personal effects when they escorted

141

me through his house to have me reconstruct my actions as far as possible, and there were no other plates among them.

Regardless of George's advice, I contacted Walter Milcross at the run-down hotel he called home, a four-story corner building on Eighth Avenue that was due for demolition soon. He was in and working on the junk jewelry he palmed off to the tourists as hot merchandise worth a lot more than the asking price, trading on people's naturally larcenous instincts. From the color TV and the new suits hanging in his closet he was doing pretty well at it.

A long time ago I had gotten him out from under a bum rap with a lot of off-duty work and he never forgot it. When I told him I wanted him to go through Argenio's apartment he looked a little startled, but figured that it would be an easy job as long as nobody was there. A quick check with headquarters got me the information that Al was out in Freeport, Long Island, processing some detail of the Scipio case and wouldn't be back for a few hours. That was enough for Walter. I told him what to look for and if anything else turned up that didn't look kosher, to hang on to it. Walter dropped his tools, picked a jacket from the closet, tucked a pair of gloves in his pocket and walked me downstairs to the corner where we split up.

I looked at my watch. It was almost one o'clock.

Overhead the grey sky that seemed to cut the taller buildings off at their middle rumbled like a tank being split and the rain filtered down to wash the arena clean enough for the slaughter to begin. I walked across town to George's building and went up to his office. He hadn't come back yet, so I went into his office and picked up his phone.

But Jerry Nolan had gotten back. The tiredness had gone out of his voice, replaced by a guarded tone. "Got something this time, Regan. Guy from Jersey City who answers the description is missing. He was an itinerant stevedore who went heavy on the booze. Just before he disappeared he was flashing a big roll around, but never said where he got it."

"How close does it fit?"

"Perfectly. He had a medical record on file with a local doctor, but no identifiable physical characteristics. His prints were in the F.B.I. file from having worked the shipyards during the war. There are police photos in the mug books and some newspaper full-length shots taken when he was arrested in a barroom brawl over there."

"It's coming, Jerry."

"You know what I feel like?"

"I know," I said softly. "It stinks. It always does."

Whatever it was, it rose up in me, that hot, tingling feeling

142

that was pure hate. My hands were wrapped into tight knots that would hardly come loose to dial another number. It was me they wanted, but it wouldn't be me they'd get. The whole skein was coming unraveled, laying itself out so you could see it in its entirety and not hidden inside a tight ball of fluff.

Ted Marker answered my ring and I knew that he had come up with it even before he said, "It checked, Regan. I found the gimmick where you said it would be and the chemical analysis nailed it. The detail assignments were in the files and he was there, all right. Do I pass this on?"

"Not yet, Ted."

"Why, Regan? Damn it, we can't let him go roaming . . ."

I stopped him. "Because that doesn't get me out, that's why."

"Hell, they can't try you again. They . . ."

Once again, I cut him off. "One more call to make. I have to find that stuff I collected on Leo Marcus. It's the only thing to shake off the negligence angle they'll slap me with at the trial. I want it all straight and in the record."

"I hope you know what you're doing," he said. "Where are you?"

"Safe enough. In George Lucas' office." I hung up.

George Lucas came through the door and piled into his chair behind the desk. He saw my face and drew back at what was written there. "Regan . . ."

"It was Al Argenio who took that shot at me. He got the silencer from one of the exhibits of confiscated weapons at the Police Academy and tried to pot me."

"Proof?" he asked simply.

"Availability. He was seen coming out when he returned it to the case."

"But he probably wasn't seen doing it. He'd make a point of that."

I shook my head and looked out the window. "He was assigned to the detail that searched the warehouse where the FS-7 and the Sentol was uncovered. He got hold of some of the stuff and delivered it to the right people for a price."

"Conjecture, Regan."

Slowly, I turned my head and looked at him. "He had made a broad a gift of stocks worth twenty grand."

George leaned back, not wanting to get too close to me for some reason. "He was on the force long enough to save that much if one of his investments did pay off. It's not impossible and it's damn near unprovable. He could claim that money came from anywhere."

He was saying things that put a sour taste in my mouth. "It was a vice with him. Some have it for gambling . . .

143

cards, the ponies . . . some have it for dames or liquor . . . he was one of the funny ones who got eaten alive by playing the stock market. It was a joke around headquarters. His paper was always turned back to the financial page."

George shook his head. "If he wore gloves when he shot you a paraffin test would show nothing. Loose stock investments would show nothing. It won't hang together, friend." He cleared his throat and went on. "If he boobytrapped your place with that sleep gas you'd need witnesses. Argenio is as much a pro as you are. He knows all the angles. He wouldn't let himself be seen. No, Pat, the only thing that will save your tail is finding that Marcus evidence in his possession."

"I'm waiting for something on that," I said. But that sinking feeling was there nevertheless. George was right. It wasn't enough, after all. I got up and stared out the window peering through the rain at the little people going to their seats to see the circus, not knowing what show was about to play and not caring either. Any show was good enough. Tomorrow the papers would headline it and they'd have a vicarious thrill at having been in the same locale where it had happened.

The phone rang sharply and George picked it up. He said something then turned to me. "For you, Pat."

I said, "Hello?"

"Walter Milcross, Mr. Regan. I'm down the street from his place. Easy job, but I didn't find nothing. Couple of stock certificates I lifted, but none of them papers. The place was clean. I would of spotted any place he stashed them only nothing showed."

All the life seeped out of me. "You're sure now, Walter?"

"You know me, Mr. Regan. Nothing in that place that even was off color outside the finger in the ink bottle."

"What?"

"Yeah, crazy, ain't it? I poked in this here inkwell . . . people stash keys in them for safe-deposit boxes sometimes thinking nobody wants to get dirtied up with ink and I pulled out a finger. A real one. Damndest thing I ever saw."

"Where is it, Walter?"

"In my pocket wrapped up in an envelope. Like maybe he's queer for fingers? I knew a guy once . . ."

"Bring it over here, Walter. You give it to George Lucas."

"Sure, Mr. Regan, but about them papers . . . you want me to . . ."

"You did enough, friend."

I hung up. The hot feeling was back. I didn't need the rest. George sat there patiently while I dialed Ted Marker. I told him what I had and told him to contact Jerry Nolan with the information. George heard it all and his face had a sickly white pallor around the nostrils. Then Ted said, "Pat . . . Argenio got back about an hour ago. He was in the file room and saw the papers with the detail assignments on them and wanted to know what it was about. Edson didn't know what was going on and told him I had requested them. I already checked around for Argenio and he's nowhere to be found. Edson said he looked like he was ready to kill somebody."

I dropped the receiver back slowly, my teeth grinding against each other. "He got wise," I said. "He's on the run."

"Where can he go?"

"Not where I can't find him."

"The trial's in an hour."

"Screw the trial. Get it postponed."

"Maybe you'd better spell it out slowly for me, Pat."

"Marcus took the Syndicate for a bundle. He proved his worth by getting Al Argenio to search my place for my documents and plant that money there."

"Argenio was being paid off by him?"

"For a long time, apparently. Who knows what favors he did. He was in a position to do plenty here and there. One of them was spotting the potential of the Sentol and the FS-7 when he was on the warehouse detail. He delivered some of it to the Syndicate through Marcus. Trouble was, he blew his wad on bad investments and always needed more. Once he was hooked by those guys he was in all the way."

"Go on."

"While I was under house arrest, Marcus used the Syndicate money to refinance the operation along the east coast. Or at least part of it. A big chunk went to his own use. He thought he could cover it later, I guess, but they don't take chances when that much is involved and double checked his accounts. When he came up short he was put on their dead list and a contract to eliminate was given to a couple of out-of-state hoods.

"Marcus got wind of it someplace . . . he probably had his own informers inside the organization, and had to cut out so both the law and the Syndicate would be off his back. He lined himself up a pigeon that looked just like himself physically. Remember . . . he had no outstanding physical characteristics. He was big and fat, bald and toothless, but no scars, tattoos or bone breaks."

"That would take time, Regan."

"Money would buy out enough time. Anyway, he found his pigeon. He promised him something, got him in his house, waited for his plan for me to go into operation because I was big mouthing about getting back at him for putting me on the hook, knowing I'd make the perfect patsy . . . and there I was.

"Hell, I wasn't hard to follow. I made no bones about what I was doing while I was on suspension. Maybe it was Argenio who tailed me, maybe somebody else. I'd like to think it was Argenio, the bastard. Marcus had been cozy with Mildred Swiss and primed her for the job. He had her standing by to feed me that Sentol. Most likely he promised her the moon and she fell for it . . . a trip to Europe with him and all the trimmings. She doesn't know what she's doing, but goes along with it, anyway.

"At that party Popeye Lewis and Edna Rells threw I was ready, the timing was perfect and I was suckered. I had one thing on my mind . . . to get Leo Marcus before the department trial came up. Once I had gotten dosed the idea really took hold and I ran off at the mouth but good. The only lucky break I had was taking six aspirins earlier. It offset one of the effects of the Sentol. Maybe I would have killed the guy who was made up to look like Marcus, I don't know. I do know I was supposed to have been found there still conscious but appearing drunk with a gun in my hand.

"Anyway, I got up those steps and was admitted inside. This part I don't remember. All I know is what did happen. I could have been carried in. When I couldn't do the job somebody . . . either Marcus or Argenio . . . took my gun and pumped six bullets into the decoy's face destroying everything he had. My gun was put back in my hand reloaded, then fired so a paraffin test would show a positive. A burned log and a dumped slug would never be found. They threw the body face down in the fireplace so the flames would burn the prints off his hands, smashed up an extra set of Marcus' dental plates and scattered the bits around and let it lie."

"What about the finger?" George asked me.

I got up and paced between the desk and the window. "That was Marcus' unfortunate accident. When the guy saw what was happening he put his hand up to protect himself and a slug took the pinky off his hand. That part was going to show when they examined the remains. A finger was missing, because Argenio found it and kept it. They had to leave a finger there for the police to find."

George looked sick again.

I said, "There are doctors around who have lost their licenses who would do the job for a price. Marcus would know them. One came up, amputated his finger, a shot was fired at the end to make it look like a bullet had done the job and the finger was wedged under the mantle. In fact, it even made

146

the case for Marcus' death better. One of his own fingers was there for the nearly irrefutable proof of his death."

"But the finger was in Argenio's place."

"Insurance, George. Al played it smart. He kept the decoy's finger and Marcus would have to keep him alive. They were both eyewitnesses to a murder they had planned and executed. Marcus had plenty on Al, now Al had the key to keeping Marcus in line and feeding him with the money he needed from the new enterprise Marcus had arranged for."

George nodded. "Then we find the doctor who did the job and . . ."

"The hell with the doctor," I said. "I want the other two. Argenio first."

"He can't get far."

It was done. Tied up. I grinned, picked up the phone and dialed Madaline's office number. She was going to be glad to hear the news. While I waited for the call to go through I told George, "Get on the other phone and start calling. There isn't time for that damn trial."

He nodded and left for the outside office as the voice on the other end said, "Sturvesent Agency, Miss Stumper's office."

"Pat Regan calling. Madaline there?"

The voice hesitated, then said, "Why . . . no. Isn't she with you?"

I had to force out the words. "Is she supposed to be?"

"But . . . an hour ago . . . there was a call from downstairs. They said it was a policeman friend of hers who wanted to see her. She said it was you and she probably wouldn't be back."

Damn it all to hell! The scene had come bright and clear in his mind and now he was pushing the destruct button. "Check that call back and get a description of the person who met her. Don't let anybody leave there until I get there. Got that?"

The urgency in my voice froze her, then she said, "Yes, sir."

At my belt the weight of the .45 was like a living thing talking to me and I ran out of the room. George was talking on the phone and I stopped him. "He has Madaline."

"Who?" George looked startled.

"Argenio. Call my office and have Jerry Nolan get an APB out and a squad working. Give him the details I gave you and hold onto that finger when Walter gets here."

"Pat . . . where are you going? Damn it, Pat, you can't . . ."

But I was out the door by then.

147

CHAPTER SEVEN

THE call had been made in the lobby of the building, relayed through the receptionist. There was no doubt about it. The description the woman at the desk gave me fitted Al Argenio, except for his pleasant manner, but he'd have to put that on to make the act effective.

He had come up behind her when she came out of the elevator and neither the woman nor the starter heard what he said, but the uniformed starter saw him take her by the arm and go outside to where a cab was waiting at the curb with the occupied flag down.

I had the receptionist put me through to headquarters and got Jerry on the line. For the sake of listening ears I turned away and kept my voice down, but it took a lot of effort. All Jerry could say was, "What the hell's going on, Regan?"

"Just listen, Jerry. I'm at the Sturvesent Agency building on Madison Avenue. Argenio got wise and beat me here. He grabbed Madaline, hustled her into a cab and took off. Alert all the cab companies and have their drivers check their trip sheets."

"How can they pull them in? They haven't got radios. Most don't break for the garages until four."

"Then put out a call to all prowl cars to look out for them. Get word to the subway guards and the tunnel and bridge attendants, but tell them to be damn careful. He'll do anything now. He's killed before and he won't stop at anything. She's his shield and a warning to me."

Jerry tried to make it sound easy, but there was an edge in his voice. "He wants back at you, Regan. He's not planning to keep her alive."

"I know," I said. "Get with it."

"We'll do all we can."

I looked at my watch. He had an hour's start. And an hour can get you pretty far from the city. One way or another, I had to locate the cab that waited for him. On the street pedestrian traffic was going by in a thin stream, hugging the walls of the buildings, leaning into the rain. The braver ones stood at the curb waving fruitlessly at cabs already filled. None were cruising. When any stopped to discharge passengers others were right there to fill it up again.

148

Madison Avenue. The center of the advertising world. The middle of everything, I thought, and I was trapped in the center of it like a helpless old lady trying to get across an intersection during the rush hour. Thousands of people were in the buildings all around me, preparing to talk commerce to the world via the medium of TV and radio and I couldn't locate a single cab for another hour yet. At four they'd break and start a new shift and I've had to wait until then.

Think, Regan. Think or she'd be dead.

I waited for the light, crossed over and half ran two blocks down to the modern, concrete structure that housed a major network studio. The head guard was a retired sergeant from the 4th Precinct I knew and when I briefed him, he led me upstairs to the right man.

Steve McDell handled special news bulletins for the radio network of the company, got my story down in thirty seconds, checked with headquarters and put the item on the air himself. Any cabbie who had picked up a fare from Madaline's building was requested to report in immediately. When he finished the broadcast he said, "It'll go out every two minutes. Let me contact the other networks in case the guy's tuned into another station."

"If he's got a radio on," I said.

"Most of them have those small transistors up on the dash these days when there isn't one installed in the car," he reminded me.

McDell flipped a switch and popular music swept into the room over a wall speaker, the continuity broken every so often by a taped rebroadcast of the announcement. Right after the third one the phones started and he answered them. "Reporters calling in," he said. "What do I tell them?"

"Nothing. They'll get a statement from the police."

He passed the message on, hanging up when they became insistent. Then one phone to his right obviously reserved for special calls blinked on, the red light on its base flicking furiously. He picked it up, talked a moment and turned back to me. "The other network. They have your cabbie on the line."

I grabbed the phone out of his hand. "This is Pat Regan, Police Department. Put him on."

There were a series of clicks as the connection was made, then a guttural voice said, "You the guy I should talk to about that call?"

"That's right."

"I just now caught it. I picked up a fare there today."

"How many?"

"Two . . . big guy and a good looking woman. He flagged me down on Forty-first, had me drive there and wait, then we

149

went out to Long Island City. I let him off right by the B.M.T. station."

"They take the train?"

"Nope."

"How can you be sure?"

"Because I turned around at the next block and they was still there trying to find another cab, that's why. I can tell you this . . . they ain't gonna get none there. It's raining like hell and all the cabs is filled. The taxi stands are empty and traffic's pretty heavy. Plenty of people waiting. You know how it is."

"Okay, thanks. We'll pick it up from there."

Steve McDell was looking at me anxiously. "Any help?"

"They're in Long Island City. I have to get there."

"Need a staff car? One's standing by downstairs."

I grinned at him. "Then let's roll." My ex-sergeant friend was caught up in the excitement like an old fire horse smelling smoke. I told him, "Call it in for me, will you?"

"Glad to, Pat."

"Get a cruiser to pick us up to clear the way. There won't be time for red lights. And tell the other networks to wipe out that broadcast. If he hears it he might jump the gun."

He caught my meaning and reached for the phone as Steve McDell and I ran out to the bank of elevators, grabbed one before the doors closed and rode it down.

The rain had turned late afternoon into near-dusk, spiked by headlights of cars picking their way through the traffic. Store fronts and office windows put on a garish display of opulence as if all were well with the world. The police cruiser met us two blocks away, cut in front and angled east, threading the way through the flow of cars with its siren.

When we reached the subway station twenty minutes later another police car was already there, parked behind a cab whose driver was talking excitedly to one of the patrolmen. I introduced myself and the cop pointed to the cabbie. "We got the call to ask around and he said he picked up a couple who answered the description of the pair."

I went over to the driver who waited anxiously. "Describe them."

He did. It was Argenio and Madaline, all right. "Dropped a fare off right at the station here," he told me. "They got in and I took 'em down to the Marco Bottling Works. That woman, she was scared, that's what I told myself. Figured like he was her husband caught her roaming. Neither one of them said nothin' while they was driving."

"They go inside?"

"How could they? The place is locked up. I was wondering

150

about it because I thought they got out at the wrong place and would need another hop somewhere else, but when I stopped at the red light at the next block I saw them in the mirror crossing the street."

"This isn't a residential section," I said.

"Yeah, I know. So where could they go? Hardly no cabs take fares from down there unless there's a direct call. Guys in the factories, they use the subway or got their own car pools."

Another prowl car pulled up and the cop beside the driver hopped out and came over. "The dispatcher's standing by for instructions."

"Blanket the area," I said. "We might have to do it building by building. Keep it quiet . . . if he knows we're this close he'll kill the woman."

"I'll call it in," he said and went back to the cruiser. The other cops got in their cars and swung out into traffic.

McDell was waiting for me, leaning out the window. "Anything you want me to do?"

"You've done enough. Stay out of it for now. If there's a story I get it to you."

"Watch yourself, Regan. Glad I could help."

"Thanks," I said. The cabbie was still standing by and I got in his hack. "Take me there," I instructed him. "Cut down the street they took. I want to look it over."

His nod was eager and he didn't bother putting the flag down. This ride was on the house, one of the things he had wanted to do all his life. If he had known all the details he might not have been so eager. The place they had left the cab was only seven minutes away. He pointed out the building, then turned left up the street he had seen them entering. Both sides of the block were flanked by structures housing small industries and businesses that couldn't stand high overhead.

Three times I had him stop when I got out and asked a few loiterers grabbing a smoke in the rain if they had seen the two of them. All I got was a negative. We kept on going, crossed the next intersection and I tried a newsstand that was behind dirty, fly-specked windows. The fat little guy behind the counter said no; until five o'clock when the factories let out nobody ever came by the place after the one o'clock lunch hour, specially on a day like that.

I was going to leave until the sallow-faced kid leafing through the comic books near the entrance muttered, "One guy came in," he muttered. "Bought cigars."

"That was this morning," the counterman said, annoyed. "Put them damn books down if you ain't gonna buy none."

Absently, I said, "Who?"

151

He tossed the books back and shrugged. "That guy with the bum hand. Got it bandaged. He got cigars."

I should have remembered. It was one of the things I hadn't had time to check before the stuff was stolen from me. Leo Marcus had used a building somewhere in this neighborhood for a drop when he was running the protection racket. "Big fat guy?" I asked him.

"Something like that. He was a baldie."

"What was with the hand?"

The kid looked up at me curiously. "He had it all wrapped up like it was broke or something."

"Ah, don't pay any attention to him," the counterman said. "He talks off the top of his head."

I took out a buck and passed it to the kid. "Buy those comic books. You earned them."

Outside, night had closed in all around us. The rain was a driving thing with clawing fingers that bit right through you, but I didn't mind a bit. The cabbie was reluctant to go until I told him to find a phone and call in my location, then he took off down the street and turned right at the corner. I walked north, looking at each building as I passed, knowing that when I saw the number it would register. The pattern was clear now. Argenio was in and he was going to use all the forces at his command to get out. He couldn't do it alone any more, knowing damn well how the department would work. Every known avenue would be cut off if he tried it alone and he wasn't up to dying slowly on the long walk to the hot seat. He had another organization with their resources to use now. Marcus could provide a way out, knowing Al had the finger that would hang a murder charge on him. One thing Al didn't know. The finger wasn't where he had left it. Later he'd try to pick it up. He might even have made it if a little professional crook like Walter hadn't known the right places to look.

I kept walking.

A couple of faces peered out the windows at me curiously.

Trucks rumbled past, the drivers intent on getting through the rain.

A wino was sprawled in a doorway, sleeping, oblivious to the wet.

The sky laughed deep in its belly and spewed another mouthful on the city.

And I saw the number 1717 and knew I was there.

It was an old dilapidated building with the front windows boarded up. No lights showed in the upper stories and the front door was locked. I went through the front door of the ornamental ironworks place next to it and an obliging guy in a canvas apron let me out the back. There was a communal area there filled with trash, a path through it leading to the electric meters on the outside of the wall. The one on the 1717 was buzzing and when I checked the rotor inside by the light of a match it was turning slowly. The place wasn't empty as it looked. Somebody was using power up there.

Above me I could barely see the vague outline of the rusted fire escape. It was within reach, but I knew the noise it would make if I tried to pull it down. Rather than try it I felt my way along the wall, found the framework of the back door and felt for the knob. It turned easily, but an interior bolt held it fast. The place was buttoned down tight, but it was to be expected. If Marcus had arranged for the place to be a hideout he wouldn't take a single chance at all. Any means of entry was probably guarded with an alarm system and probably up there he had another escape exit ready if he had to use it.

One window shone dully in the light close by. Time was ticking off too fast, and I couldn't go probing for other ways of getting in. I stood there trying to decide what to do and the sky was ripped apart by a brilliant streak of lightning.

Then I knew what I was going to do.

When the thunder came with a shocking crack of sound I rammed my elbow through the pane and no fall of glass could be heard above the reverberation of nature at all. I picked the shards out of the frame, and when there was room to get through, felt for the wires of the signal system, located them and slid inside.

Leo Marcus should have updated his alarm setup. It was the old style dependent upon the raising of the window to activate it. I stood inside getting used to the deeper darkness, the .45 cocked in my hand. Little by little I felt my way across the room and into another, careful where I placed my feet so that a stray sound would carry upstairs.

One room opened into another filled with stored furniture I had to edge around. Once I had to hold a stack of chairs that nearly toppled, then I got them balanced again and circled to the door. I pulled it open slowly, timing the squeaking of the hinges to the rumble of traffic from the street. Enough light came in the front windows to outline the hallway and the staircase that led to the floors above.

I stayed close to the wall where there would be less chance of hitting a creaking board, taking every other step, diminishing the chances of touching one wired to the alarm circuit. My hand felt for trip wires, found one and I stepped over it, grinning silently in the darkness. Other people knew the tricks too.

I looked into one room on the second floor where all the desks were, the windows painted black, then didn't bother with that floor at all. I went up the next flight, ran into a duplication of the trip wires down below and got over them. Once a board creaked ominously and I paused, waiting to see if there would be a reaction.

None came and I knew why it didn't.

From someplace on the next floor came the muffled sound of a woman's screams and it covered any sound I made getting to the top. She screamed again and I located the sound behind a steel door studded with rivets, a barricade only a dynamite charge could break down.

My mouth muttered impotent curses and I didn't give a damn any more. I struck a match, saw another door at the end and ran down to it. Behind the steel she screamed again and somebody laughed. I recognized Argenio's voice.

This door wasn't steel. The tongue of the lock on the inside ripped loose from the dry rotted wood when I threw enough pressure against it and I shoved it open, then closed it behind me. Another match reflected off a black painted window and guided me to it. I found the alarm switch at the top of the frame, threw it into the off position, unlocked the catch and pried the window up.

Under the window a four-inch ledge ran the length of the building. Not wide enough to walk, but enough to give me one vital step that would put my hands within catching distance of the fire escape that was outside the other room.

I hated to do it, but I needed the cover. I didn't know what they were doing to her or what it cost her, but I needed another scream wrung from her mouth. I waited, poised, heard that muffled laugh, barely audible, then the piercing note of a scream that barely reached me.

I jumped.

For a second I thought I'd lost it, but my fingers hung on and I dragged myself up and over the rail and reached for the .45 before it could fall out of my waistband. I stood there outside the window and she screamed again. The sound barely penetrated. I struck a match, saw myself reflected in the black of the window, but through a scratch in the paint saw the planks that covered it from the inside.

The entry had to be quick. There had to be a diversion, enough to rattle them. Surprise was gone now, but a diversion would work. One of the steel slats that formed the floorwork of the fire escape landing was loose at one end and it only took a minute's work to work it loose, one end breaking with a shallow hook on it like a crowbar.

From his seat in the coliseum, the old man with the scythe

roared with pleasure at my tactic in trying to beat the game and applauded with a clap of thunder. I got the curved edge between the two windows, snapped the catch when he clapped again, then eased the window up.

The bell went off inside, a high-pitched, tinny sound that came from outside the room. Through the crack in the boards I saw part of a man run past, heard the stifled curse, then kicked the board in with my foot and ducked my head into the opening to stare at the hideously grinning face of Al Argenio.

For a fraction of a second time had ceased, but in that millisecond he read my eyes and saw everything come apart and knew that there was nothing left unknown at all. He had her tied to a chair with her clothes torn from her body and had been giving her a sample of the things he had always taken pleasure in and now enjoyed even more, trying to force confirmation from her just to be sure the game had been played out the old way, and ready to kill her when he was certain of it and start a new one behind Marcus.

But I hadn't told her anything and she hadn't been able to talk. Now I *was* telling him things. Silently. The Sentol, the FS-7, the silencer, the finger in the ink bottle . . . and now it was over. He read the whole message in my eyes and fired from the hip.

He didn't even come close. The .45 punched a hole at the bridge of his nose and left a stream of matter from the floor to the wall and he was whipped onto his back by the force of the impact, dead before his body hit the boards.

It only took a couple of moments to kick a hole through the opening, wrenching the boards loose. Downstairs somebody was yelling for somebody else to call the cops and a beam of light flashed up to where I was going through the slats.

Only one fluorescent light hung from the ceiling casting a bluish pall over everything. The blood that oozed from Madaline's mouth had a purple tinge and the welts across her breasts and shoulders from the leather strap he had used were a dark maroon. Her eyes were dull, glassy with pain and fatigue, then she recognized me and the light came on behind them.

To one side a door stood open where Marcus had disappeared, but I wasn't chasing him now. He wasn't going anywhere. Outside in the city the sirens had begun to sound the last chord and they'd know who to look for.

I dropped the gun in her lap and began working at the knots in the rope that held her. "Easy, honey. Relax."

First one untangled, then another and her arms fell limply

to her sides and I knelt down and started on the ones that bit into the flesh of her thighs and calves.

She squirmed, went rigid. I looked up to tell her not to fight against the pressure, then I saw her face. Fear had drawn it tight and her mouth was half open in a soundless yell of warning.

Leo Marcus said from the doorway, "All right, Regan, just stand up and turn around."

I swung my head and saw him, the gun in his good hand, the bandaged one held clutched to his stomach. His eyes were wild and alert, his mind racing. I let my hands drift over my head and stood up, taking a step to shield Madaline from his fire.

They'll be here soon, I kept thinking. I could hear them coming. He could get me, but they'd get him. At least she'd stay alive.

Marcus could read my face too. "No good, Regan. There isn't enough time."

"There's no place to go, Marcus."

"I have a way out," he said simply. "It's been prepared ahead of time. I'll be on my way while they're still trying to figure this one out."

"They know, *Marcus*."

"Do they?" His eyes mocked me.

"They have that finger to prove it."

He made a vague gesture with the gun. "Anybody can lose a finger. Don't forget . . . they have mine, too."

Damn him anyway! He was right. It wasn't conclusive.

"I like this approach even better now." He glanced at the body of Al Argenio, then back to me. "Now he's out of the way. You two had a shoot out, that's all. Incidentally, this is his gun. I think it will work very nicely. Everybody knows of the hatred between you two. The woman was the crux of the matter. She was caught in the middle when you shot each other." He laughed softly. "A simple matter of putting a gun in his hand. Even my former . . . er, associates will buy the picture."

"You've had it, Marcus," I said, stalling.

He shook his head. "I should have done this a long time ago. It would have saved a lot of trouble to do it right there in my own living room." He raised the gun and sighted along the barrel.

Her whisper was almost soundless. "Move, Regan."

I took one step as the shot burned past me, tugging at my coat. Somehow the .45 slug from the rod she held squeezed in both fists tore the gun from his hands taking fingers and

156

all, leaving a great, gouting stump dangling from his coat sleeve.

Leo Marcus looked down at the obscenity that had been a part of him a second ago, opened his mouth in what started to be a great bay of absolute horror and collapsed in the agony of frustration and pain.

The sirens were close now. They were stopping and voices were yelling instructions. I took the gun from her hand, put my arm around her and got her to her feet. Her coat was in the corner, and I draped it around her as they were coming up the stairs.

In the doorway Leo Marcus' life ran out of him in a swampy pool of arterial blood and nobody was going to know anything except what I wanted them to know.

Madaline's face was still ashen white, but the color was coming back into it. Outside I heard Jerry Nolan's voice calling for axes to smash down the door. She said, "Is it over, Pat?"

I kissed her gently and shook my head. "No, kitten, it's just beginning."

Other Outstanding **Suspense Novels**
in SIGNET Editions

☐ **A DOOR FELL SHUT by Martha Albrand.** A concert violinist is drawn into a whirlpool of deceit, violence and feverish adventure in this novel of murder and intrigue set in divided Berlin. (#T3331—75¢)

☐ **THE WIDOWMAKER by M. Fagyas.** An enthralling suspense novel, based on fact, about a Hungarian village at the close of World War I where husbands are no longer needed and are dying off mysteriously one by one. (#T3282—75¢)

☐ **ODDS ON by John Lange.** A unique mystery, in which three ingenious gentlemen utilize an IBM computer to mastermind a million dollar hotel heist. (#P3068—60¢)

☐ **A QUEER KIND OF DEATH by George Baxt.** A new kind of detective makes his debut in a turned-on mystery, the swinging story of a queer kind of murder in a queer kind of crowd. (#P3188—60¢)

☐ **THE FEBRUARY DOLL MURDERS by Michael Avallone.** Tackling a Communist spy ring with a plot to sabotage the U.N., private-eye, Ed Noon, finds himself unwittingly transformed into an espionage agent upon whose shoulders depends the freedom of the entire world. (#P3152—60¢)

☐ **DRAGON HUNT by Dave J. Garrity.** A dazzling debut for private-eye Peter Braid—rugged and relentless, fast with guns or fists, and even faster with women. (#P3203—60¢)